I0734458

Resurrection of Hope

By

Tamera Lynn Kraft

Mt Zion Ridge Press

http://www.mtzionridgepress.com

ISBN: 978-1-949564-22-8

Copyright © 2015

Published in the United States of America
Publish Date: February 1, 2019
Cover Artist: Gwen Phifer

Cover Art Copyright by Mt Zion Ridge Press © 2018

All rights reserved. No portion of this book may be reproduced or transmitted in any form or by any electronic or mechanical means, including photocopying, recording or by any information retrieval and storage system without permission of the publisher.

Ebooks are *not* transferrable, either in whole or in part. As the purchaser or otherwise *lawful* recipient of this ebook, you have the right to enjoy the novel on your own computer or other device. Further distribution, copying, sharing, gifting or uploading is illegal and violates United States Copyright laws.

Pirating of ebooks is illegal. Criminal Copyright Infringement, *including* infringement without monetary gain, may be investigated by the Federal Bureau of Investigation and is punishable by up to five years in federal prison and a fine of up to $250,000.

Names, characters and incidents depicted in this book are products of the author's imagination, or are used in a fictitious situation. Any resemblances to actual events, locations, organizations, incidents or persons – living or dead – are coincidental and beyond the intent of the author.

Dedication and/or Acknowledgement

I dedicate this book to my husband Rick Kraft who, like Henry, is a good man with a great heart. I love him very much and would be lost without him.

Chapter One

Palm Sunday, 1919

Tonight would be the last time Vivian Klein cleaned Mr. Adder's office. After she finished for the day, she'd take the Colt handgun she'd seen in the top drawer of his desk and finish off her miserable life.

Tomorrow morning, the owner of the Greenville Hotel would find her dead body sprawled beside the desk on his fancy wool rug. A certain satisfaction set in as a grin crossed her face. He'd have to find somebody else to clean away the blood.

First, she needed to finish her chores. After washing dishes and changing sheets, she started scrubbing the narrow linoleum floor in the second-floor hallway. She tackled the scrub brush with a relish she hadn't felt before. These constant tasks taking over every moment of her existence for the last six months would soon end.

It wasn't like this had been the worst day of her life. A year ago, she had received a telegram informing her James, the love of her life, had died in the Great War. She paused for a moment, leaning on her heels, the memories flooding her emotions.

"Soon, my love. I'll join you soon."

Setting aside the heartache, she wiped away a tear and got back to work.

Footsteps shuffled down the hall and stopped abruptly as the fetid scent of cigar smoke mixed with the sweet smell of lilac aftershave assaulted her senses. A prickle crept over her like ants crawling all over her skin. She dropped the scrub brush and stood to face Mr. Albert Adder. She kept her disdain at bay as she looked down at him.

The owner of the Greenville Hotel, dressed in a dapper three-piece suit and bowtie, stretched his neck and shoulders reminding her of a rooster trying to crow, but it didn't add one inch to his short stature. He glowered up at her over his bifocals and pointed nose, his dark eyes betraying the deviousness within. "I hope you've reconsidered my offer," he said, his characteristic smirk in place. "I only want to improve your situation."

The knot that never left Vivian's stomach tightened. "If you really want to help me, you could start by paying me a decent salary."

Adder ran his hand over his balding scalp. "I give you room and board. Nobody else came to your aide when you were left destitute. You should be grateful."

She dug her fingernails into her palms to keep from smacking his face. If he hadn't introduced her father to alcohol and gambling in the hotel's back room, she wouldn't have lost the farm. The room still operated even though prohibition had already been enacted in Ohio. "I'll never marry you."

"I know I'm a bit older than you…"

A snort escaped Vivian's lips.

"Lots of men marry younger women. Be reasonable, girl. If you agree to be my wife, you won't have to work so hard. You'll have everything you ever wanted." He touched her arm.

It took everything inside not to cringe. She tilted her chin up with the last vestige of self-respect she had. "I won't change my mind."

Mr. Adder's lips pressed together. "Fine then. If you want to be a scrub woman for the rest of your life instead of the wife of the richest man in town, so be it." He stomped down the stairs and out of sight.

She tried to pick up the scrub brush but couldn't get her trembling hand to cooperate. *Please Lord, if there's another way.*

It was a useless prayer. God hadn't come to the rescue when James was killed. Or when she cared for her sisters and parents as they died of influenza. Where was He when the sheriff showed up at her door and told her she had twenty-four hours to leave the only home she'd ever known?

God had deserted her. It was time to end it.

*****

Henry Bauer's stomach felt like a flock of birds had taken flight as he made his way into Resurrection of Hope Church in Stillwater Village, Ohio. He couldn't wait to see a glimpse of Vivian Klein, the woman he hoped to spend the rest of his life with.

Like the town he'd grown up in, the church hadn't changed

since he'd been off fighting in the Great War. A brick building with a bell tower held rows of wooden pews with hymnals at each seat. The cross stood tall behind the wooden pulpit in the front, and the anxiety bench, where he gave his life to God after his mother died, rested near the pulpit.

Deacon Roth started the service with the opening prayer as Henry slipped into the back pew. He kept looking over his shoulder to see if any latecomers arrived, but the door never opened. After singing a couple of hymns, he barely squeaked out the chorus. The words caught in his throat. Vivian wasn't coming.

He squelched the urge to leave while everyone was still standing so he could try to find her. He didn't even know where to look. The day he got back, the first thing he did was to march to her house with a bouquet of daisies he'd picked on the edge of his farm. He had knocked firmly on the door. When it opened, a man he'd never seen stood there. Another family lived there now. They bought the property at the sheriff's auction, and they had no idea where to find Vivian.

Reverend Krieger came to the pulpit and spoke with his usual deep resonating voice, giving the same Palm Sunday message he had every year since Henry was a boy. None of the military chaplains conducting church services in the trenches brought the Bible to life like Reverend Krieger.

Henry had looked forward to hearing him preach, but he couldn't manage to pay attention. He focused on the chip in the stain glass window then the gouge in the wooden pew in front of him. The walls needed a fresh coat of paint. Maybe blue, the same color as the dress Vivian wore when he last saw her at the train station. She looked pretty in blue.

Vivian was out there somewhere maybe needing him.

As soon as the service ended, he rushed over to the reverend before the line to greet him formed.

"Henry, my boy, it's so good to see you back safe. I was so sorry to hear about James. I know you and he were close, almost like brothers."

Henry tried not to interrupt, but his anxiety got the better of him. "Reverend Krieger, where's Vivian Klein staying?"

"The girl James was going to marry?"

Henry nodded.

The reverend wiped his hand across his bushy mustache. "After she received notice of James' demise, she stopped attending church. I tried to visit, but she refused to see me. Her father asked me not to come back. You know her folks never did cotton to anything about God. I think they had a hand in keeping her away."

The muscle in Henry's jaw twitched. "So, do you know where she is now?"

"No, I haven't the foggiest idea. Her folks and sister died a couple of months ago during the influenza epidemic. It was a sad time. Stillwater Village lost near twenty souls."

"Yes, I know." Hardness formed in the pit of his stomach as the flock of birds lodging there turned into bricks. She was out there somewhere, alone. "When I went out to the farm, she'd moved away. The people living there hadn't ever heard of her."

"Must have been the Morgans. They moved into town a few months ago."

Henry tugged at his bowtie.

"Things were so dreadful then with the quarantine and all the deaths, it took me a couple of weeks before I could get out her way to offer my assistance." The reverend cleared his throat. "By then, Sheriff Berg sold the farm at auction and sent her away. Something about a mortgage and taxes not being paid. I wish I could have done more."

Henry thanked Reverend Krieger and scanned the faces of the congregation. There had to be someone here who knew what happened. Jeff and Rose Weber stood by the doorway. They lived a couple of miles outside of town on the farm next to his and were so busy with farming and raising their eight children, Henry doubted they had time to keep track of the whereabouts of their neighbors.

Some others had surrounded Abe Zimmer as he enthralled them with tales of bravery from the Great War. Already popular because of his good looks and exploits on the community baseball team, Abe was now an acclaimed hero after winning a couple of medals.

He wouldn't have any information on Vivian either, and Henry felt awkward interrupting his war tales even if most of them were as full of hot air as a German Zeppelin was hydrogen.

Mrs. Oster stood near the coal furnace talking to a group of women. She was the doctor's plump wife who always wore her hair secured in a gray bun and rarely closed her mouth. Because of her husband's job, she pretty much knew everything happening in Stillwater Village. Doctor Oster did some doctoring at the county seat in Greenville. Maybe they'd seen Vivian there.

Henry shuffled in toward them. He wasn't much for chitchatting with people he didn't really know, especially a group of gossiping older women, but if anyone knew where Vivian had gone, it would be Mrs. Oster.

When he reached the cluster, they jabbered away without even a glance toward him. Men like his friend James and the town hero Abe Zimmer commanded attention by their very presence, but Henry blended into the crowd. He was never noticed, and until now, and that was the way he wanted it.

He cleared his throat.

The ladies startled like he had miraculously appeared in front of them.

"I'm sorry to bother you, ladies." Henry glanced at his polished shoes and hoped they'd detract from the frayed cuffs of the sack suit he'd pulled out of his trunk when he packed away his doughboy uniform. He'd lost weight in the army, and the way the ladies looked at him made him feel like a boy wearing his father's clothes. He cleared his throat. "I was wondering if you know the whereabouts of Vivian Klein."

Mrs. Oster stepped forward. "You look familiar, young man, but I don't recollect your name."

"Henry Bauer, ma'am. James Wagner's friend."

Hope Hahn, a petite woman with smiling eyes, answered. "Oh, yes. I remember you. Henry, isn't it?" She turned to the other ladies. "Henry has the farm down the road from my sister and her husband."

"Yes, ma'am." He tugged on his bow tie.

Mrs. Krieger patted his arm. "Sad to hear about James. He was a good man."

"Yes, ma'am." Why couldn't they just answer his question?

"Seems to me," Mrs. Oster said as she tapped her chin, "the last time I recollect seeing her was when my husband treated a boy at the hotel over in Greenville. She got a job there after Sheriff

Berg sent her away."

Heat rose to the back of his neck. "The Greenville Hotel?" She couldn't be working there. Not after the way Adder got her father to take up gambling. Vivian had talked to him often about it. "Are you sure, ma'am? The one on Washington Avenue?"

"Of course, I'm sure," Mrs. Oster said. "Wouldn't have said it if I wasn't sure."

"Yes, ma'am." Henry tipped his hat to the women and headed to the door. He didn't have time to put up with any more of their idle chatter. If Vivian was working at the hotel, she needed him to save her from that man.

The ladies didn't even wait until he was out of ear shod to make him the topic of their conversation. "Strange boy, that one," Mrs. Oster said. "He and his pa never said more than two words to me before."

Henry didn't mind the comment. He never had any reason to talk to her before now, and he doubted he would ever start a conversation with her again.

He strode out of the church and slipped into the driver seat of the new 1919 Model T he'd bought a couple of days earlier. It took a good portion of his military pay, but he still had plenty left to buy seed and a few animals. The days of horse and buggy travel were coming to an end, he wanted a vehicle he could rely on. He'd hoped the shiny new black car would impress Vivian more than his sloppy suit and show her he was capable of supporting her.

He drove to Greenville and parked on the road in front of the hotel. He sat there for a moment and swallowed hard at the lump in his throat. Vivian loved James, not him. He always knew it. That's why he never told her how he felt. She deserved James, or somebody like him. What if she refused his proposal?

His whole body grew heavy, and he couldn't seem to lift his arm to open the door. He remembered holding James' hand as he died, his last words to Henry, "Take care of Vivian," a promise Henry intended to keep even if it meant risking her rejection. He got out of his automobile and marched into the hotel.

Adder glanced up from the newspaper on his desk. "What can I do for you?"

"I want to talk to Vivian Klein."

"She's on duty." He dismissed Henry with a wave of his hand and went back to reading his newspaper.

"I know." Henry kneaded the back of his neck. "I need to talk to her."

Adder glared at him and crossed his arms.

"Now." Henry's voice bellowed through the lobby. This one time, he risked drawing attention for Vivian's sake.

"She's not allowed visitors." Adder stepped out from behind the lobby counter and blocked the path to the rooms.

Henry brushed past him and strode through the faded green hallway toward the rooms. "Vivian! Vivian!"

"Now, see here." Adder rushed after him and pulled on his arm, but he pushed it away. "If you don't leave, I'll call a policeman."

"Do what you have to do." Adder rushed off, and Henry reached the end of the hall and climbed the narrow staircase. "Vivian." He saw her, and it took his breath away.

Knelling in the landing at the top of the staircase with a bucket and a scrub brush beside her, she looked up. Even with her auburn hair strung in a braid down her back and her faded cotton dress soaked with soapy water, she was beautiful. "Henry Bauer." Vivian stood, her brown eyes widening. "What are you doing here?"

He climbed the staircase two steps at a time until he reached her side. "I heard what happened. I want to help."

She blew a stray hair away and wiped her forehead with her arm. "You want to... Nothing you can do."

His face flushed. "You don't understand." He knelt to one knee. "Marry me."

She let out a snort. "You're talking foolishness. I can't marry you."

"Yes, you can. I know you love James, but your feelings for me will grow. Let me take care of you."

*****

Vivian tried to hide how startled she was at Henry's proposal. Of course, she remembered the quiet boy who she and James had been best friends with since childhood. He was always tall and skinny, but with all the weight he'd lost, he looked like a scarecrow. She wasn't sure she liked his short army haircut. It didn't seem like Henry for him not to have an unruly mop of dark, curly hair falling in his eyes.

"Why would you want to do a foolish thing like marry me?"

Henry's hazel gaze became intense as he started to reach out to touch her then drew back. "I was with James when he died. His last words to me were, 'Take care of Vivian.' I've always been fond of you." He bit his lip and looked away.

Vivian touched his arm. "It's not fair to saddle you with a wife because of this promise you made."

"I don't have anyone left. I want a wife and a family. I promised James. Say yes."

He made it sound so easy, and his pleading eyes compelled her to agree, but they didn't love each other. "I can't, Henry. It wouldn't be right."

"I don't know how you could say that." Henry tipped back on his heels and gave her a slight grin. "People have been getting married for centuries without love entering into it. We are friends. Isn't that a good start?"

"I don't know what to say. I'm not ready to even think about caring for anyone else. I'm still grieving James."

"If you give me a chance, we can make this work." This time Henry did hold her hand. "We'll marry, and you can move into my place. I'll provide for you, but we'll have separate bedrooms. I'll give you the time you need. When you're ready to be my wife…" He blushed. "I'll give you the time you need."

Vivian touched her chest. Her breathing shallowed until she'd become lightheaded. This couldn't be the answer to her earlier prayer, could it? Could it be the way out? "Can you give me time to think on it?"

Henry grinned. "I'll be back tomorrow." He descended the stairs and turned down the hallway until he ebbed out of her sight.

His footsteps clacked against the wooden floor, the sound of hope shuffling back into her life.

She wiped the tears from her face. She didn't even know why she was considering this. He didn't love her, and she didn't love him. Henry was always in the background, not the kind of man you considered marrying. Maybe she could learn to care for him that way.

When he came back tomorrow, she would say yes.

Chapter Two

Vivian sat in the wooden pew at the back of the church biting her lower lip as Henry explained the situation to Reverend Krieger. She hadn't been here since Palm Sunday a year ago, the day she found out about James.

The church felt the same, wooden pews with a center aisle leading to the anxiety bench on the right and a Kenwood upright piano on the left. A wooden cross hung in the middle of the wall. A few years ago, Vivian prayed at the bench while starring at that cross knowing God would take care of her.

A shudder went through her. This church felt too much like a safe refuge, and it scared her. If she'd learned anything in the last year, there was no place of safety, not even in God.

Standing near the piano, Reverend Krieger glanced in her direction then listened to Henry with a somber look on his face. This wasn't how it was supposed to be. She should promise to love, honor, and obey James, not his best friend.

A silly grin appeared on the preacher's face. She didn't know what Henry said, but somehow he convinced Reverend Krieger that this was a normal wedding between two people who wanted to be married to each other.

Mrs. Krieger, who had darted outside as soon as Henry had announced their intentions, ran into the church with some wildflowers she must have picked from the front lawn. "Wait." She handed them to Vivian. "Can't have a wedding without flowers."

"Thank you." Vivian drew the black-eyed Susans to her nose and took a whiff even though they had a faint scent. The yellow flowers always reminded her of daisies, her favorite flowers. The lump in her throat grew. Mrs. Krieger's kindness broke through the wall she'd built to keep her heart from being crushed again. She worked at holding back the tears.

Grabbing her by the hand, the preacher's wife led her to the double doors. "I'll play the wedding march, and you walk down the center aisle." Mrs. Krieger headed toward the piano.

"Now, dear," Reverend Krieger said through that smirk of his. "They don't want all the trimmings. They just want a simple ceremony."

"Nonsense," Mrs. Krieger said. "This is Vivian's wedding day."

Reverend Krieger gave a shrug. Mrs. Krieger clanked *The Wedding March* on the out-of-tune piano.

Vivian sauntered to the front, flowers in hand, not sure if she was promenading into a sunny future whose warmth might heal her fractured soul or a cyclone ripping apart what was left of her heart apart.

Glancing at Henry, she almost felt like a real bride. She glanced down. The green cotton dress she wore was nothing like the wedding dress she planned to make.

Henry had a look in his eyes she'd never noticed before, a softness she might have mistaken for love if it had been James standing there. He gave her a reassuring nod, and when she reached the front, he took her clammy hand, and she didn't pull back.

The music stopped.

"We are gathered here today in the face of this company, to join together Henry Bauer and Vivian Klein in matrimony, which is an honorable and solemn estate and therefore is not to be entered into unadvisedly or lightly, but reverently and soberly."

Heat coursed through Vivian. What did Henry say to Reverend Krieger? Did he know this wedding was not being entered into reverently? Would God be angry at her for going through with this?

"Into this estate these two persons come now to be joined. If anyone can show just cause why they may not be lawfully joined together, let them speak now or forever hold their peace."

Everything in her wanted to run, to forget this scheme of Henry's. This wasn't a real wedding. It was making a mockery of what she and James had planned. What was she thinking agreeing to it? Only Henry's gaze stopped her from scampering away. It was so intense and yet tender. She held her peace.

"Henry, do you take Vivian for your lawful wedded wife, to live in the holy estate of matrimony? Will you love, honor, comfort, and cherish her from this day forward, forsaking all others, keeping only unto her for as long as you both shall live?"

"I do." The catch in his voice almost convinced her he meant it.

"Do you, Vivian, take Henry for your lawful wedded husband, to live in the holy estate of matrimony? Will you love, honor, comfort, and obey him from this day forward, forsaking all others, keeping only unto him for as long as you both shall live?

"I do." It came out as barely a whisper.

The preacher pronounced them man and wife and declared Henry could kiss his bride.

Henry's breath shrouded her face as he leaned forward. She closed her eyes waiting for his lips to press against hers. When their mouths touched, her body trembled and her knees threatened to no longer hold her weight. She wanted to lean into the kiss and, at the same time, recoil from it.

Henry drew back leaving her even more confused. Feeling the lingering pressure, she touched her mouth with her fingers.

Reverend Krieger shook Henry's hand, and his wife hugged Vivian.

Henry took her arm. "We best be going."

Vivian allowed him to lead her to the car. It was a warm spring day, but a chill went through her. His kiss promised more than a marriage of convenience. What if he decided to go back on his promise and demand a wedding night?

She escaped Mr. Adder's advances with this charade, but now, how would she evade her husband, the man she didn't love?

The man who didn't love her.

*****

Henry wasn't sure how to sort out the whirlwind of emotions stirring inside him. He'd married the woman he'd loved since he was a child, but it was a marriage in name only.

He drove them to Greenville after the wedding so they could have supper in the restaurant, but during the meal and on the drive to his farm, she hadn't said a word to him. He understood why.

After promising he wouldn't make overtures toward her, the first thing he did after they were pronounced man and wife was to kiss her. He didn't know what possessed him to lean forward and kiss her. It amazed him she didn't slap his face. Maybe she was too surprised.

He couldn't help himself. Even in a simple cotton dress holding those yellow flowers, she took his breath away. She always had. He let up a prayer he would have more self-control. Vivian had been through so much. He didn't need to scare her with his desires. If he was patient, she would grow to love him.

After parking his Model T next to the porch, he got out and opened the door for her. "We're home."

She looked up at the old farmhouse but kept quiet. As children, they talked so easily with each other, but now, awkwardness hung between them as if they had just met.

"I have lots of plans for the place." Henry opened the front door and led her into the parlor. "The old sofa needs new slipcovers, and the armchairs are threadbare.

He tugged at his bowtie. He should have thought to replace the chairs. "I received some back pay from the army, and I have a savings my father left me. So anything you want to do to fix the place up is fine."

She nodded but didn't say anything.

"I was planning to get indoor plumbing put in." He didn't know why he was talking so much, more than he ever had in his life, but he couldn't seem to stop. "I know it's an extravagance, but I'm keeping back enough money for seed and such."

He led her to the kitchen. At least it had a pump in the sink and large cupboards. "This is the kitchen." What a stupid thing to say. Of course, it was the kitchen.

Vivian opened cupboard doors and the icebox and ran her hand along the old coal-burning stove. The start of a smile crossed her lips, but no words formed.

"We can get one of those new-fangled gas stoves if you like. They have a few in Greenville."

She shrugged.

He led her to the small room next to the kitchen where a claw foot bathtub resided. "This is where you'll…" Heat flushed his face. "Bathe. I'm planning to install a water closet as soon as the crops are planted so you won't have to go to the outhouse."

"Henry, I have no right to say anything." She bit her lip. "I don't think you should spend all your savings on these new gadgets. Why don't we put some back, and we can worry about indoor plumbing after you harvest the crops. If there's enough."

A dark red curl fell in her face, and he squelched the urge to push it back. "If that's what you want, might be wise to wait."

She gazed directly at him for the first time since he kissed her. A light sparked in her dark eyes. "I don't need all those fancy things. This is better than I've ever had."

Henry nodded. "I want you to think of this as your home now. You have every right to say how you think things should go."

She blushed, but her stony silence returned.

"One more room to show you." He led her past the staircase to the largest bedroom at the back of the house, the one where his parents slept.

The day before he'd gone looking for her, he had tried to make sure everything looked nice. He'd dug out his mother's doilies and set them on the dressing table and had made the bed with his mother's cotton sheets and log cabin quilt.

A new portable Singer sewing machine and cabinet set in the corner near the window. He'd paid extra to take the department store model. He didn't want to wait six weeks to have it delivered. Vivian had always liked to sew, and the store clerk at department store in Greenville said it was the best machine they sold.

As she stepped inside the room, Vivian's gaze focused on the bed. Her eyes widened.

Henry stammered. "This is your room. I'll sleep in my bedroom upstairs."

Her shoulders visibly relaxed. She walked to the sewing machine. "Would it be all right to buy some material to make a few dresses and maybe some slipcovers for the sofa and chairs? I could even make you a new suit." She blushed. "One that fits."

"I'll take you into town tomorrow."

"That would be nice." She gazed at him, tilted her head, and opened her mouth slightly, but whatever she planned to say next never made it past her lips.

"I'll get your carpet bag out of the automobile so you can get settled." Henry placed his hand on the doorknob and paused. "I'm glad you're here."

He wanted to say more, but he didn't.

Chapter Three

Vivian twisted one of her long curls as Henry parked his Model T on the side of the road in front of the Stillwater General Store. She hadn't been in here since the sheriff foreclosed on her parents' farm and sent her away with little more than a couple of dresses and some personal belongings stuffed in a carpetbag. The thought of seeing anyone who knew what happened made her stomach churn.

Stillwater was a small village with only one store in the center of town that doubled as the post office. A gas pump stood out front for the farmers who'd traded in their horse and buggies for Model T's. Doctor Oster's office was across the road with his house next door. A little farther down were a two-classroom school, the sheriff's office, and a grain elevator.

Maybe she could find what she needed for her sewing projects, and she could get in and out of the General Store without anyone noticing.

Henry offered to travel to Greenville to shop, but Vivian refused. Even going to the restaurant on their wedding day had made her on edge. If she saw Mr. Adder again, she wasn't sure how she would manage. Even worse, how Henry would react.

When he'd came to rescue her. Mr. Adder had threatened to have him arrested for abducting his employee. Vivian's heart had raced faster than a barnstormer's airplane when Henry grabbed Mr. Adder by the shirt.

The gold flecks in Henry's hazel eyes flashed. "You don't want a scuffle with me, Adder. I know what you do in that hidden room of yours."

Adder sputtered. "How... you can't... I..."

Henry let go of him and straightened his jacket. "Vivian, let's get out of here."

Vivian had never seen anyone get the better of Mr. Adder before, but it convinced her she had made the right decision. She was still grieving for James, but she could see herself eventually falling for a man who would protect her like that.

They stepped into the store, and Vivian's hopes were dashed. Everyone in Stillwater Village had chosen this morning to do their shopping.

Half a dozen men stood around the checker table discussing the Dodgers trading Jake Daubert and the communist plot to mail bombs to US politicians. Doctor Oster, a fan of President Wilson's handling of the Red Scare, seemed to have the most to say, but Hank Andrews' red face and pounding on the table showed he was as passionate about his opinion.

Mr. Johnson, the middle-aged storekeeper proud of his slicked back hair and a handlebar mustache, pulled down a sack of flour for Mrs. Oster while four other ladies waited with lists in hand.

Other women looked through yard goods, and three boys gathered around the toy shelf oohing and awing over Mr. Johnson's marble collection and baseball gloves. The small store barely had enough room for all the customers, and with the unusual heat wave they were having, the humid air seemed in short supply.

Nadine Norris set down a bolt of white satin and scurried to them first. "Vivian, Henry. So good to see you." She gave Vivian a short hug. "It's the talk of the town how you two up and got hitched without telling anyone."

Vivian liked Nadine. A perky girl with blue eyes and the latest bobbed hairdo, she always managed to make people feel at ease even if she did talk too much. "We didn't really have a chance to tell anyone. It happened so fast."

"It's so romantic," Nadine said. "I told Abe we ought to run off and elope, but he wouldn't hear of it. Says since he's the sheriff and all, it would only be fitting."

Henry crossed his arms and leaned against the wall. "Abe is the sheriff now?"

"Yes, silly. When he got back, Sheriff Berg offered him the job. Said he wanted to retire and move to Ravenna where his aging mother lives. Since Abe was a hero and all, the sheriff figured he could handle himself."

Vivian barely had time to process the relief she felt at never having to see Sherriff Berg again when Henry gave Nadine a tight nod and began to look through the farm tools displayed in the corner.

"Look what Abe gave me when he proposed." Nadine held out her hand and flashed her new diamond ring. "He wants me to have a big church wedding with a satin dress and veil and all the trimmings. After all, I am marrying the most important man in Stillwater Village."

Before Vivian could respond, Rose Weber, Hope Hahn, and some other young women from the village surrounded her and gave her hugs. A lump formed in her throat, and she clutched her purse tighter.

"Vivian, land sakes, it's really you." Rose, the younger sister, was short and a little on the plump side, probably because of birthing her eight children. A couple of years older than Vivian, she had married young and didn't wait to start having babies. One arrived every year keeping track with the calendar, and it looked like number nine was on the way. "I heard you married Henry Bauer. He's so shy I didn't think he would ever propose to anyone."

"Me either," Hope said. Thinner and shorter than her sister, she had never managed to have children. "I was sure he'd die a bachelor."

Nadine held out her hand. "Did you see the ring Abe bought me?"

Rose took hold of her hand and inspected it. "You're going to blind me with the thing." She let out a sigh and placed her hand on her stomach. "Looks like love is in the air this spring."

Vivian glanced toward the bolts of material. "If you ladies will excuse me, I do need to pick out some material. I don't want to keep Henry waiting too long."

All three women turned their heads and gawked at Henry, still ogling the farm equipment, like he was Houdini magically appearing before them. Henry had a way of blending into the surrounding without being noticed, like a chair or a sofa table. Sometimes Vivian envied that trait in him. Like now.

Hope placed her hand on Vivian's arm. "We know things haven't been easy for you with your fiancé being killed in the war and your whole family dying of influenza, Sherriff Berg had no right to evict you like he did. He could have talked to the bank and asked them to give you some time. We want you to know we're here if you need us. None of what happened was your fault." She wiped her eyes with her pink embroidered handkerchief.

Vivian didn't know what to say.

Rose stepped in. "What we're trying to say is we really are happy for your marriage and, well, everything. We have a sewing bee every Tuesday at my house after lunchtime. We sure would like you to join us."

Vivian's voice thickened. "I don't know." She presumed they would shun her and gossip about her, not invite her to their sewing bee. Instead, they offered her their friendship. She blinked to keep tears from spilling out.

"Please say yes," Nadine said. "You're the best seamstress in town, and I really do need your help with my dress."

Afraid her voice would betray her, Vivian nodded.

The ladies excused themselves, and Henry's enthrallment with the tools waned. He turned and glared at Vivian. "Best get the supplies you need so we can get back home. I have some plowing to do."

"All right." She made her way toward the sewing supplies. Maybe Henry didn't approve of her buying so much. That could explain his curt tone. "I could just buy enough for one dress and a couple of work shirts to start."

Henry rubbed his hand across the back of his neck. "No, that won't do. I don't want to have to come back in town every time you need something."

She bought enough yard goods to make slip covers for the living room, three to four day dresses and one church dress along with enough for some work shirts for Henry. She already had in mind what style to make the church dress. She'd make a navy blue frock, hemmed three inches above the ankle, with a double row of white buttons on the front, a wide white collar, and a white sash around the middle. It would be the prettiest dress in Stillwater Village and convince Henry he made the right choice for a wife.

Henry tucked the purchases into the back before cranking up the car and applying the choke. They were half way home before he spoke. "I saw you with those ladies in the store."

"They were so nice to me. They even invited me to their sewing bee on Tuesday."

"Best we keep to ourselves. You don't need to be traipsing around all the neighbors stirring up trouble."

"Stirring up trouble!" Heat rose up her back. "You don't own me, Henry Bauer. This isn't even a real marriage. I'll go where I please with whom I please."

"You vowed to obey me, and I'm against it."

Vivian dug her nails into her palms as she stared out the window at the corn fields they were passing. She wouldn't let him see her cry.

*****

Henry could see from Vivian's reaction he'd said the wrong thing. She didn't say another word the whole way to the farm. When they did get home, she ran into her bedroom and slammed the door. It was almost suppertime, and she still hadn't come out.

He drummed his fingers on the table trying to figure out how to fix things. Why was she so mad? He had just warned her it was better to keep to themselves. The sooner she learned that, the easier it would be.

His stomach churned. With the mood she was in, he probably wouldn't get any supper unless he made it himself. He got out a frying pan and searched through the cupboards trying to decide what to cook. Heavy footsteps sounded behind him. He turned around.

Vivian glared at him with her arms crossed. Her brown eyes had grown darker. "Since we were going into town, I made cornbread earlier." The words came out caustic. "And some pinto beans. I'll warm them up."

"Wait." He took her hand and directed her to sit at the table. "What's wrong?"

"What's wrong?" She sputtered. "What do you think is wrong?"

He rubbed his hand across his mouth. "If I knew, I wouldn't ask you."

"You can't keep me locked up in this house away from the outside world the way Mr. Adder did. I don't care if I am your wife. I won't have it."

Henry rubbed his temples. "I'm not trying to lock you up. I'm trying to protect you."

"Protect me? From a sewing bee?"

"The best way to stay out of trouble is to not nose around in other people's affairs. I've tried to live my life that way."

She leaned back in her chair. "What you're saying doesn't make sense. You've been James' friend for years, and if you hadn't meddled in my life…" The muscle in her cheek twitched. "Your meddling saved me in more ways than one."

"I miss James." He swallowed hard at the lump in his throat. "He was the kind of friend a man could depend on, and it got him killed."

"What do you mean?"

He rubbed his thumb over the knot on the oak table. "Nothing."

Vivian touched his hand. "Please, tell me. I need to know."

A sour taste settled at the back of his throat. Maybe it was better she knew now even if she didn't forgive him. "I never was a good soldier, but I tried. Somehow I wound up in the middle of no man's land and lost my sense of direction." He rubbed his legs as sweat beaded his forehead. "Guns blasting from both sides, and I didn't know what to do. James came out of nowhere and led me back to our trenches, but before we could climb in, a machine gun opened fire. They got him. I dragged him in, but it was too late." A thickness settled in his throat. "If James hadn't tried to save me, he'd still be alive."

Vivian threw her arms around him as a sob escaped her.

A flush shot through him as he tried to figure out what to say. After a moment, he patted her back. "I'll tell you what. If you want to go to the sewing bee, I won't stop you."

She drew back, and tears welled in her eyes.

He pulled out his handkerchief and handed it to her. "What did I say wrong now?"

"Nothing." Vivian wiped her face and made her way to the cupboard. "I'm just grateful you were with James when he died."

Henry shook his head as she heated up their dinner. His mother was like that, all teary-eyed for no reason. He couldn't figure it out, but he vowed he would treat his wife kindly. His dad had no call to berate his mom every time her emotions spilled out. He'd never treat Vivian like that.

He took a couple of plates off the shelf and set them on the table. "I figured after supper we could read a few verses out of the

Bible and pray together. That's a habit I want my family to get into."

Vivian glanced toward him, and by the look of her flushed face, he was afraid he'd primed her pump again. "No need for me to be talking to God. You can pray for both of us if you want."

Henry swallowed. "You believe in God, don't you?"

"Yes, but God is mad at me. No sense in making things worse."

"What makes you think that?"

Vivian let out a snort. "I used to read my Bible and pray and was in church every time the doors were open. Then God took away James and let my family die. I lost everything. If it hadn't been for you, I don't know what would have happened."

Henry touched Vivian's arm. "Who do you think sent me to rescue you?"

The tears started again. "Please don't." Vivian ran into the bedroom and closed the door.

Chapter Four

Thrusting the masher into the bowl of potatoes, Vivian had the urge to dance around the wooden table in the center of the kitchen. Today had been the third sewing circle meeting she'd attended, and she already finished all of her dresses including her navy-blue church dress. She couldn't wait for Henry to see it.

They'd been getting along better, and their friendship had renewed itself. Lately, some of the feelings Vivian had when she watched Henry plowing the field went beyond companionship.

She set the pork chops, mashed potatoes, and peas on the table and called out the back door. "Supper's on."

Henry set down his plow and wiped his forehead with his bandana. "Be in as soon as I wash at the pump."

It was a hot day, and he'd taken off his shirt. The beads of sweat on his muscular forearms made Vivian's knees wobble.

She was tempted to let him know she wanted to consummate the marriage, but she wouldn't yet. He'd made it clear when he married her, he was doing it out of his friendship for James.

Until he wanted her as his wife, she wasn't about to obligate him. When she showed him her new dress, maybe he'd start to see her as more than a charity project.

Henry sat at the table, and after saying grace, dished a healthy portion of food on his plate. The man knew how to eat. After gnawing on his pork chop and eating a few bites of mashed potatoes, he stopped long enough to grunt. "This is good."

Vivian grinned as he went back to eating. "I finished sewing my church dress today. I can't wait for you to see it."

He set his fork down and scowled at his peas. "That's right. The sewing circle was today."

She let out a sigh. "I don't know why you're so sour on it. I need time with other women, and you know how I love to sew."

"I guess." Henry drew a bite of mashed potatoes to his mouth. "You can show me the dress after supper."

She wanted to wrap her arms around his neck, but instead she ate a forkful of mash potatoes.

Henry didn't offer any more to the conversation until he shoveled the last bite of apple pie in his mouth and downed his last cup of coffee. "Go try it on. Let's see what it looks like."

She nodded, hurried into the bedroom, and changed. If anything would allure him, this dress would do it. The sash showed off her small waistline, and the narrow skirt showed her hour glass figure. She checked herself in the mirror, pinched her cheeks, and bit her lips to brighten them up.

Parading into the parlor, she twirled to show off her new creation.

"That's nice." Henry sat in his overstuffed easy chair facing the fireplace and opened the newspaper in front of him.

"Nice. That's all? Just nice?"

He set the paper down and looked at her like a puppy who didn't understand why it was being sent outside after peeing on the floor. "I said I liked it."

She sank into her wooden rocking chair with blue flowered cushions she'd sewn to match the slipcovers she'd made for his chair. "I'm going to wear it at Nadine and Abe's wedding. She asked me to stand up for her."

The muscle in Henry's cheek twitched. "No wife of mine is attending Zimmer's wedding,"

The pork chops she'd eaten had turned into bricks in her stomach. "Of course we're going. Why wouldn't we?"

"Don't you remember?" He hoisted to his feet, knocking over the lamp. He reached over and caught it before it hit the floor.

"Remember what?"

He rubbed his hand across his face. After an awkward moment, he sat and propped his elbows on his knees. "Abe Zimmer. I should say Sherriff Abe Zimmer. That day down by the creek?"

Vivian let out a slight gasp. "Oh."

Abe was about three years older than her and used to run with a gang of rowdy boys. When she was ten years old, she had been walking near Stillwater Creek picking blackberries. Abe and a couple of boys had come by and started tormenting her. One of the boys knocked over her basket of berries, and another pulled one of her braids.

Her heart raced. She glanced around wondering if she could

outrun them.

"Don't be treating her mean," Abe said as he inched closer. "She's a pretty one." He leaned toward her, grabbed her around the middle, and tried to press his lips against hers.

She turned her head and screamed as loud as she could. The other boys came to Abe's side, but Abe just chuckled.

"Leave her be." Henry appeared out of a patch of trees like one of those knights of the roundtable in a book she'd borrowed from her teacher.

Abe glared at Henry for a moment, then let go of her arm. "Come on, guys. She's not worth it." He and his gang took off on the path toward town.

Her knees gave way, and Henry caught her before collapsed to the ground. She sobbed, and he held her until she calmed down. "It's all right," he said. "I won't let anyone hurt you."

Abe had never bothered her again, but he did cause distress for others. When he was fourteen, he stole some pies and turned over tables at the church picnic. Sheriff Berg threatened to throw him in jail, but after Reverend Krieger had a long talk with Abe in private, everything calmed down.

Nobody knew what was said in the reverend's office, but Abe never caused trouble again. He spent the rest of the summer whitewashing and cleaning the church.

He changed in other ways too. He worked so hard in school that he was ranked salutatorian at graduation. James was valedictorian. Later Abe became the head pitcher on the town's baseball team and had become James' friend.

"That was so long ago." Vivian played with a stray curl as she tried to think of a way to break through Henry's mood. "Abe's changed a lot since he got religion. There has to be another reason."

"People like Abe Zimmer don't change. My advice is to stay out of it. If you really want to help Nadine, tell her not to marry our new sheriff. Either way, we are not going to the wedding."

Vivian blinked back the tears. "I better change and get to the dishes."

Every time she felt she might love him, he had to do something to ruin it.

*****

Henry sat in his chair in the living room with new blue flowered slipcovers Vivian had made and pretended to read his newspaper. It was hard to concentrate on the labor riots in Cleveland with all the noise in the kitchen. Pots banged, and at one point, he was certain she'd broken a plate. The worst part was the tears.

There has to be another reason.

Vivian had figured that much out, but he couldn't tell her the rest of why he would never trust Abe Zimmer. Or anyone else in Stillwater Village.

The only man he'd ever told was James.

Abe hadn't let things drop after Henry came to Vivian's defense. At school, he threatened to beat up anyone who dared eat lunch with Henry. After class, Abe and his gang surrounded him, hurling insults at him most of the way home.

Henry would have punched Abe in the jaw, but Abe's friends outnumbered him. He didn't want to explain to his father why he had bruises or a black eye and risk a worse beating than Abe and his friends could give.

One afternoon, Abe went too far.

"I can believe Darwin's theory, Henry, 'cause your mom looks like an ape."

Henry's heart pounded in his ears. He lunged toward Abe. The others descended on him, and their fists landed in his face and body, but he didn't feel any pain. He was too focused on striking his fist into Abe's jaw.

Shouts sounded, and arms pulled him away. Abe and his friends ran off leaving him in the dirt tasting blood from his cut lip. The next thing he knew, James Wagner stood over him offering him a hand to help him on his feet. He accepted James' help, and they'd been best friends ever since.

The only argument they'd ever had was after Abe supposedly changed. James tried to convince him to forgive, but he would never let go of what Abe did. Or excuse himself for what happened.

A loud crash came from the kitchen followed by loud sobs.

He pressed his lips together and let out a silent prayer. He loved Vivian with all his heart and would do almost anything for her, but she was asking too much trying to get him to go to Abe's wedding. Why couldn't she trust he knew what was best?

He rubbed the back of his neck. Keeping his wife cooped up in the house without letting her out to socialize was like keeping a wild animal caged. She was too much like James, friendly, outgoing, full of life.

His mother used to be like that, but after years of his father's berating, she retreated inside herself. After a while, her friends stopped dropping by. Henry didn't fault her for abandoning hope. Why hadn't he done something to save her?

Squaring his shoulders, he marched toward the kitchen. He wasn't going to end up like his father and suck the life out of his wife. When he opened the kitchen door, she sat on the floor in the middle of shards and pieces of a broken plate, sobbing.

He knelt beside her. "Vivian." He touched her cheek.

She looked up at him with her doe like eyes. "I didn't throw the plate if that's what you're thinking. It slipped through my fingers."

"Shhhh, it's all right." He leaned forward. He wanted to kiss her but didn't dare. "I'm sorry. I didn't mean to make you cry. You can go to the wedding."

She wiped her face. "You'll go with me?"

"I can't." He clenched his jaw. "Please don't ask me."

"All right." Vivian stood, sniffled, and brushed off her dress.

She was pretty even in her day dress with the oversized muslin apron, but the blue church dress she had modeled for him earlier made her look like one of those actresses in the moving pictures in Greenville.

She caught him staring at her, and he flushed.

Crossing her arms, she scowled. "You can't keep me from going places and seeing people. You might be a hermit, but I'm not."

Henry nodded. The scent of dish suds and Ivory soap along with her soft brown eyes made his heart race. He cleared his throat. "I'll get the broom and dustpan for you."

It wouldn't hurt to let her visit with neighbors and go to social gatherings as long as she didn't get after him to go with her.

He handed her the broom, and when their finger touched, an electric charge filled the room. All the air rushed out of his body as he stammered. "I best get back to my newspaper."

He dashed into the living room without another word. She shook him to the core of his being, and he wasn't sure how much longer he could evade her charms.

She'd called him a hermit, and maybe she was right, but if he wanted to keep his promise to keep their marriage one of convenience until she was ready, he needed to keep his distance.

He would become a hermit with her as well.

Chapter Five

When Vivian come out of her bedroom wearing her new church dress with her hair in curls, Henry's heart raced faster than the freight train running through town. He seized the newspaper and held it in front of him to keep from getting another glimpse of her. She was so alluring.

He could feel her staring at him, but he didn't dare lower the paper.

"It's such a beautiful day for an August wedding. Are you sure you won't come with me?" There was a longing in her tone.

"No, you go along. I'll be fine."

"Henry." She pushed the paper down to where he could see her face. "You need to get out and meet our neighbors. The only place you ever go, other than the store to pick up supplies, is church, and you never talk to anyone but Reverend Krieger."

He clenched his jaw. Why couldn't she leave it be? "It's best if we keep to ourselves."

Vivian groaned, snatched the paper, and tore it into pieces. A smirk spread over her face, and she dumped them over his head.

The muscle in his jaw twitched. His heart pounded like a steam locomotive's engine, and before he knew what he was doing, he stood and gripped her by the shoulders.

The look of fear in her widened brown eyes startled him. Shaking his head, unable to believe what he'd done, he let go and slunk into his chair. "You better get going. You'll be late for the wedding." He didn't know how he calmed his tone so quickly, but his words came out steady and detached.

She pressed her lips together and took a step toward him. He tensed preparing for the angry words he deserved. Instead, she spun on her navy-blue pumps and stormed out of the house, slamming the door behind her.

When the door crashed shut, Henry's hand trembled. He hadn't been so afraid of losing control since the day his mother died. Why did Vivian have to provoke him like that? She acted like she wanted him to get angry.

He went to the pump at the kitchen sink, wet his bandana, and placed it on the back of his neck.

Hadn't he tried to give her the time she needed? He kept his distance, barely looking at her, afraid it would churn passion inside. When they sat at the table for meals, he would answer her questions but avoided anything that would start a conversation with her.

When they were in high school, James, Vivian, and he would go to James' baseball games together, and after James joined his team before the game, Henry had time to be alone with Vivian. Conversations with her back then came so naturally. Most people would try to pry words out of him, but she didn't mind the silence until he'd formed in his mind what he wanted to say.

During those dialogues in the bleachers, he realized he was in love with her, but after what happened with his mother, he wasn't sure he ever wanted to get that close to someone.

When James told Henry how he and Vivian had fallen in love, all Henry felt was relief. Now he could keep them both in his life without committing to more than friendship.

James was the type of man Vivian deserved. Popular, likable, good at sports and school and just about anything else he put his mind to. Henry never understood why James wanted to be his friend, but he was a good one, and Henry was grateful for him.

When James asked him to look after Vivian in his dying breath, Henry couldn't walk away. The more he prayed about it, the more he knew he loved her too much to desert her.

Maybe he shouldn't have married her. She wasn't happy, and when he got too close, the temptation to make her his wife in every way was overwhelming. In the morning, she smelled like fresh baked bread. When he came in from working on the land, she would have the best suppers he ever tasted laid out on the table.

Then in the evening, while she sat in the rocker with a needle and thread, her auburn hair glowed in the lantern light, and her large brown eyes warmed the cockles of his heart. She didn't realize what she did to him.

Today was the hardest when she came out of her bedroom with her hair fixed in curls wearing her best church dress. He almost relented and told her he would go to the wedding with her.

With the weight of regret pressing on his chest, he made his way back to his easy chair and plunked in it. Even if he wanted to, he couldn't have escorted her. There might be dancing. He didn't know how he would control himself if he had her in his arms on the dance floor.

It had scared him when the rage his father displayed came out in him. Toward her. He loved her so much, but he didn't dare show it.

He couldn't go on like this with his heart burning inside his chest. The dam he built around himself to keep his emotions from flooding out was about to burst. Since he wouldn't allow it to come out as love, anger spilled over instead.

Vivian didn't deserve this hurt and loneliness he'd trust upon her. There had to be something he could do to spend time with her and not give in to his desire. She talked about wanting to see the moving picture *Daddy Longlegs* with Mary Pickford. Taking her to a picture show and to eat afterwards wouldn't be too difficult. They'd be in public the whole time, and it would make her happy.

He'd ask her as soon as she got home from the wedding.

First, he needed to make things right.

*****

Vivian sat alone at the table near the front of the large tent set up outside the church watching couples dance around her.

Rose sat beside her, took a few labored breaths, and patted her full tummy. "This little one won't let me dance for long. I get too tuckered. Jeff's getting me some punch."

"You need to be careful," Vivian said. She couldn't think of a better reply.

"I suppose you'll be in the family way soon. By the way, where is your husband?"

Vivian smiled to keep the hurt from showing on her face. "You know Henry. He's not much for socializing."

Jeff came over with two glasses of punch. After giving one to his wife, he set the other in front of Vivian. "I figured you might need this since your man isn't here to fetch it for you. Wouldn't he come out to the wedding?"

Vivian took a sip of the punch. "He's not much for weddings."

Jeff pulled on his collar. "Can't say I'm much for getting dressed up in this monkey suit either, but Rose wouldn't hear of me staying home. Guess Henry's the lucky one to have such an understanding wife."

Rose gave him a playful swat.

Jeff ignored it. "You tell Henry I'll be coming by. The men and I were talking about doing some repairs on the school, next Saturday. Some shingles came off in the last storm, and we need to get it done before harvest time."

Vivian's stomach knotted. She could imagine the reception Jeff and his friends would receive. "Not sure Henry has time for that."

"Well, I'll stop by anyway."

"Suit yourself." Vivian took another sip.

Hope stopped by the table. "Wasn't Nadine's dress pretty?"

"Prettiest wedding dress I've ever seen," Rose said. "Other than yours, dear sister."

Hope blushed. "I tried it on the other day. I can still fit in it. Isn't that something after ten years of marriage?"

"It's 'cause you don't have children to ruin your figure," Jeff said.

Hope's eyes watered, and Rose stood and put her arm around her sister while delivering a glower toward Jeff.

Jeff looked apologetic. "I'm sorry, Hope. I wasn't thinking."

Vivian excused herself and meandered around the tent. Mrs. Oster strode toward her, and her heart skipped a beat. She thought about walking the other way pretending she didn't see the doctor's wife, but it was too late.

"I'm so sorry Henry couldn't come, dear," Mrs. Oster said. "What kept him away?"

Vivian plastered the fake smile on her face. "He's not much for weddings."

"No man is." Mrs. Oster fanned herself with a Greenville Funeral Home fan. "Most put up with them for their woman's sake though. I have half a mind to have a heart-to-heart with that man, allowing you to attend this wedding on your own."

"No, please don't." Vivian placed a hand over her stomach. "I'm all right with him staying home."

"Oh, dear." Mrs. Oster patted Vivian's hand. "You two didn't have an argument, did you? I'm so sorry."

Vivian swiped at the tear rolling down her cheek too late to hide it from Mrs. Oster. "I'm sure most newlyweds quarrel. We'll be fine."

"Of course you will. If there's anything I can do, you just let me know." Mrs. Oster strode off before Vivian could answer.

Her knees wobbled as she sat on the wooden fold-up chair and pinched her nose to keep from shedding anymore tears. With women twirling around her in their husbands' arms, she felt so alone, but she didn't leave. Home was the last place she would feel loved or wanted.

It was a mistake to marry Henry. She realized that now. When she baited him by tearing up his newspaper, he didn't even have enough passion for her to get angry. He had a moment of irritation about his newspaper when he grabbed her, but there wasn't enough fire in him to go any further.

How could she believe anyone could love her like James did? Maybe it was best to end things now.

She didn't bother to say her goodbyes on her way out the door. They were too busy having fun to notice anyway.

At least Henry let her use the Model T. She wouldn't have to walk home in the dark. As she pulled on the starter and choke to get the engine running, thunder roared in the distance. Another storm brewed.

She drove home rehearsing what she would say. They weren't right for each other. It was better to end this now before they had a real marriage. If he would let her stay for another month until she found a job and a place to live, she'd pay him rent with her first paycheck.

She swallowed the lump in her throat. What if he wanted her to leave right away? She couldn't go back to Mr. Adder. She'd become a railroad tramp first.

Rain beat against the windshield, and Vivian turned the crank for the windshield wiper. The sound of thunder and rain somehow calmed her. The sky sympathized with her trouble.

As she pulled the car in front of the house, she wiped tears off of her face and took a deep breath, bracing herself for what she needed to do. She ran to the porch as the rain beat down then timidly opened the front door.

Henry stood there with a grin, holding daises, and looking very much like a little boy. A handsome full-grown little boy. It was the first time she noticed his hair had grown back from his army cut. The curls hung in his eyes the way they used to when they would talk at James' baseball games. She cared for him so much then, for both of them.

He handed her the flowers. "I'm so sorry I acted the way I did. If you'll forgive me, I promise I'll do better."

"I don't know what to say." It was the truth. This was the Henry she cared about, the man who had been a good friend when she needed one.

"Don't say anything. Let me make it up to you. How about we go to the Saturday matinee in Greenville and see the new Mary Pickford moving picture?"

"I'd love that." It was better to end it like she planned, but the same hope she felt when he came to the Greenville Hotel seeped back in her heart.

Chapter Six

Henry and Vivian sat at a back table at the Greenville Restaurant eating apple pie and drinking coffee. It was the nicest day Henry ever remembered.

"Mary Pickford was wonderful," Vivian said between bites of pie. "It was so romantic when she found out the man she loved was her benefactor. She's so pretty. What did you think about her cutting her hair short?"

He took a sip of coffee to hide his grin at her enthusiasm. "I didn't really notice."

"You didn't notice?" She took a sip of coffee. "That's the style now. Even McCall Magazine shows women with short hairdos. I was thinking of bobbing my hair."

"So are you going to sew dresses with short hemlines, turn down your stockings, and wear a lot of jewelry and bright red lipstick too?"

She set her cup down. "You're making fun of me."

"Not at all. I think you'd look adorable as a flapper." He leaned back in his chair and imagined what she'd look like with short hair. "As long as you don't take up smoking."

"You don't have to worry about that." She curled up her cute little nose. "I hate cigarettes and cigars. I'm glad you don't smoke."

"Never saw the need to take it up."

"Henry, this had been a wonderful day, but I could have waited until next week if you wanted to help the men at the school."

A lump formed in his throat. "How did you know? You were inside the house when Jeff stopped by."

"He told me when we were at the wedding. Helping the community is important. I would have understood."

"Nothing to understand." He cleared his throat to make sure his tone didn't sound harsh. "I'm sure there were plenty of men to take my place, Abe Zimmer for one. Best I stay out of it. I have plenty to keep me busy around the farm."

She stared at her empty plate and didn't say any more.

He was such a fool. They were having a great time, and he had to ruin it talking about their new sheriff. He placed his hand over hers. A stirring churned inside of him. "Besides, I wouldn't have missed this date for anything."

A smile replaced her pensive stare.

"Would you like take a walk, maybe look in some of the shops around town before we head back?" Henry asked hoping to change the topic. The truth was he didn't want this day with her to end.

"That would be lovely."

After placing a nickel tip on the table, he stood, pulled out her chair and made his way to the counter to pay the bill.

The bell on the door clanged, and Albert Adder strode in with a young girl hanging onto his arm. The girl, dressed like a flapper with bright red lipstick and rouge on her cheeks, couldn't have been older than eighteen. Henry put his wallet in his pocket and placed a protective arm around Vivian as they passed the misfit couple.

"Well, well, look who's here," Adder said.

"Come on, Vivian." Henry pulled her closer as he approached the exit.

"It's the hick farmer and his wife." Adder turned to the girl. "I offered her the world, and she turned me down for this ruffian."

Heat shot up Henry's back, but he didn't respond to the jeers. He needed to get Vivian away from that snake.

When they got outside, he turned to look at her. "Are you okay?"

"You were wonderful." She hugged him, and he wasn't sure he wanted her to stop. She pulled back but left her hands resting against his chest. "Thank you for keeping me safe from that man and for not making a scene."

"With that bonehead? He's not worth it." He gazed into her eyes. Every nerve in his body felt a charge going through him, urging him to take her in his arms and kiss her in the middle of East Park Avenue. He cleared his throat "I hope he didn't ruin your day."

"No, not at all." She looked down then back at him. "It's such a beautiful day after all the rain we've been having. Instead of shopping, let's take a walk through McPherson Park."

"That would be nice." He took her arm in his and headed toward the park.

A clanging filled the air as the Dayton Interurban streetcar passed by. They strolled past the red brick store fronts and crossed the tracks. A large buckeye tree guarded the entrance to the park, and Henry swept the buckeyes, large two-toned brown nuts, aside with his foot. They meandered down the path.

Vivian's words flowed as she described how her mother and father were always arguing and how her father rarely came home for dinner because he was in Greenville gambling.

She stopped and leaned against a white oak. "I don't want things to be that way with us. I want us to be able to have dinner together every night and discuss things with each other without the meanness."

Henry placed his hand on the tree above her head and leaned in. "I want that too." Her lips drew him in, and he wasn't sure he could resist the temptation they offered.

"If you mean that, then will you try paying attention to me? Sometimes you act like I'm not even there."

A warmth surged through him. If she only knew…

"Henry, do you hear what I'm saying?"

He cleared his throat and stepped back. "Yes, but I'm not very talkative."

"I know you're quiet. That never stopped us from discussing things before you went off to war." She bit her bottom lip. "I've been trying to be a good wife. I've painted the living room and made slipcovers for the furniture. I make sure you have good meals waiting for you when you're done in the fields. I've done everything I know to do. It would be nice if you would, I don't know, just notice I'm around like I'm important to you."

"You're the most important person in my life." They started walking toward the pond, and he slipped his hand into hers. She didn't pull it away.

"I'm the only person in your life."

Ducklings crossed the path in front of them, following their mother to their swimming hole.

Henry stopped and clutched her shoulders. "I mean it. I don't know what I'd do without you." He took her in his arms and kissed her.

He expected her to jerk away and slap him, but instead she leaned into the kiss and parted her lips. His heart raced as he let go of her and gingerly pulled back.

"A good start." She blushed. "I want to be your wife in every way."

"I want that too. Are you sure?"

"I'm sure."

"Let's go home."

*****

During church the next morning, Vivian tried to pay attention to Reverend Krieger's sermon about how faith and hope are intertwined, but her mind kept flittering back to the night before. Henry was so kind and loving. It was a perfect wedding night.

She glanced toward him and blushed. He didn't seem to have any problem keeping focused on the message. She envied that.

Before she realized it, Reverend Krieger said the benediction, and the service ended. Henry locked her arm in his and stood in the line to greet the pastor. Sherriff Abe Zimmer approached them and tipped his hat.

Henry's Adam's apple bulged.

"Great weather we're having."

Her husband nodded. "What do you want, Sheriff?" His tone had an edge to it.

Sheriff Abe rubbed the back his neck. "I know I'm not your favorite person though I've tried to make things right on my end."

"Get to the point."

"This isn't about me," the sheriff said. "This is about the community we live in. I noticed you weren't helping at the school yesterday. Can I ask why?"

Henry crossed his arms and glared at Abe. "I don't see it's any of your business. Unless I've broken some law."

Vivian placed a hand on his arm hoping her presence would somehow help.

Abe let out a heavy sigh. "Look, I know you don't want to be my friend, and I respect your privacy. I'm not trying to start trouble, but we weren't able to finish the school yesterday, and we need to get that roof done before it rains. Every able-bodied man in town is going to join me in the morning and get it done."

"What does that have to do with me?"

40

Henry's set jaw showed her there was nothing she could do or say to get him to change his mind. She had to try. "It wouldn't hurt to take one day out to help at the school."

The look he gave her caused her to back up a step.

"Look," Abe said. "We need everyone's help if we want to get it done in one day."

Vivian swallowed and let up a prayer Henry would listen to reason.

"I won t be there," Henry said. "Best you ask some of the other men who have time for such foolishness."

"If that's the way you feel, I won't trouble you about it anymore." Abe's eyebrows lowered and pinched together. "But chew on this. Someday you'll need help from your neighbors, and I hope to God they don't feel the same way." He tramped away without even bothering to shake Henry's hand.

"Let's go, Vivian."

She rushed to keep up with him as they raced past the line and the reverend on their way toward his Model T. She slunk into the passenger seat. A heaviness settled over her. Why did he have to act like such a fool?

He had been a good friend to James, willing to do anything for him. She remembered once when James' horse broke his leg and he didn't have enough money for another one. He needed that horse to get work at Bear's Flour Mill. Henry gave him his horse. Told him not to worry about paying him back. Henry said he knew James would do the same for him.

It wasn't only with James. He had shown such kindness with her, not only saving her from Abe's advances when she was a young girl or rescuing her from Adder but waiting until she was ready to be a wife to him. Why couldn't he be that way with their neighbors?

Henry started the car and drove toward home, his jaw set, his eyes focused on the road ahead of them. "Don't ever do that to me again. I won't stand for you disrespecting me in public, you hear."

"I'm scrry." She blinked back the tears.

He handed her his handkerchief but didn't look her way.

She wiped her eyes and passed it back to him. "Why can't you help them? I could do the chores around the farm. The crops won't be ready to harvest until next week. Besides, our children will go to that school."

"The subject's closed."

Vivian didn't say any more. Somehow she had to find a way to get through to her stubborn husband.

Chapter Seven

Henry shouldn't have talked so sharply to Vivian. It was ruining his appetite. If only she could understand how he felt about getting involved with the neighbors. It would lead to nothing but trouble.

He'd braced himself for an afternoon of her sulking or banging around pots and pans, but she didn't seem too upset after the first few minutes. For Sunday dinner, she even fixed his favorite meal of fried chicken, mashed potatoes and gravy, and apple pie for dessert. He loved her cooking.

All of this civility shook him more than any grumbling would. It was like waiting in the trenches for a battle to start and not knowing when the mortar would fall. He picked at the mashed potatoes until he had enough of it. "Vivian, I shouldn't have spoken to you the way I did."

"It's all right." She wiped the corners of her mouth. The disagreement hadn't hurt her appetite. Everything on her plate had been eaten. "I don't think you're right, but I shouldn't have said so in public. I'm the one who should apologize."

Henry gazed into her eyes trying to see if she meant what she said. He couldn't find any guile there. "I wish I could make you understand why it's better to stay away from our neighbors."

"Let's not say any more about it." She stood and cut two pieces of apple pie. "We'd better finish our dessert. We need to hurry if we're going to have devotions before the evening church service."

Henry's mouth dropped open. He had never mentioned including her in his daily devotions since she made it clear she didn't want any part of it.

A smile crossed her lips. "Don't look so stunned. I never said I didn't believe in God."

"You could have fooled me."

She got his Bible and sat at the table beside him. "What I said was God is mad at me. Lately I'm wondering if maybe I was wrong, so I asked Him for something I knew only He could do."

"What did you ask for?"

"Not telling." She ate a bite of apple pie. "It wouldn't be a fair test if you know what it is."

Henry shook his head as he turned to the page where his ribbon marked Luke chapter 10. He read out loud about Jesus sending out his disciples and about how he rebuked the Pharisees before reading the story of the Good Samaritan. "But he wanted to justify himself, so he asked Jesus, 'Who is my neighbor?'" He cleared his throat.

Vivian touched his arm. "Would you like me to read the rest?"

He took a sip of coffee. "Okay."

As she read the story about the Samaritan helping the man on the side of the road, Henry pulled at his collar. Why did that have to be the passage for tonight's reading?

Sweat beaded his forehead as she finished the chapter. "'Which of these three do you think was a neighbor to the man who fell into the hands of robbers?' The expert in the law replied, 'The one who had mercy on him.' Jesus told him, 'Go and do likewise.'"

He wiped his forehead with his handkerchief. "It's a hot day."

Vivian put the Bible on the shelf and grabbed her hat, gloves, and purse. "I don't think so. It's nice to have a breeze for a change."

*****

It was all Vivian could do to suppress a chuckle at church that evening when Reverend Krieger announced his text for today was "Who is my neighbor?" and started preaching on the Good Samaritan.

It was too big of a coincidence to believe this wasn't God answering her prayer. She cautioned herself it might have had nothing to do with her asking God to prove He loved her. The real test would be if her stubborn husband decided to help with the school without her nagging him.

She glanced at Henry. Poor man looked like he had swallowed one of her pins.

As soon as the last prayer ended, Henry didn't even wait for her. He sprang from his seat and fumbled his way outside.

She did her best to follow, but Rose stepped in the way.

"Vivian, could you do me a favor?" Rose asked.

"I will if I can."

"I'm in charge of providing lunch for the men building the roof for the school." Rose fanned herself with a funeral home fan. "It looks like every man in town is going to be there. Could you help with preparing the meal?"

Vivian bit her lower lip. She wanted to help no matter what Henry decided, but she wasn't about to let him accuse her of disrespecting him in public again. "Can I let you know?"

"I don't know how." Rose crossed her arms. "You know I don't have a telephone."

"Neither do I but…" Vivian tried to think of a way to tell Rose her husband didn't want to help with the school without making him look bad. If God didn't change his mind, she couldn't go without him. Could she?

She let up a silent prayer. "I'll be there. Do you want me to bring anything?"

Rose grinned as if Vivian had agreed to single-handedly create world peace. "A bowl of potato salad would help."

"I'll bring it." Vivian excused herself and made her way outside. God had to come through, or when she got home, they were going to have an argument making the Great War looks like a family squabble.

She scanned the parking area and found Henry standing under the oak tree in the front yard with Archie Hahn, Hope's husband. Archie's bushy mustache twitched as the men talked, and the cheeks on his round face puffed out.

Why did her man have to cause trouble? Why couldn't he just agree to help with the school?

Her face grew hot as she gazed at the white clouds wisping through the sky. *God, where are you?*

Henry shook hands with Archie, ran his fingers through his unruly hair, and strode toward her. Vivian didn't a word as her heart shrank. She should have known better than to trust God to answer her prayers. Henry opened the door for her, and she scooted in.

On the way home, she tried to think of a way to tell him she'd be at the school whether he was there or not. Her insides quivered as she shifted in her seat and clutched her purse. He would accuse her of disrespecting him again.

She squared her shoulders but didn't look his way. "There's no other way to say it. You might be too stubborn to help the community fix the school's roof, but I'm not. I told Rose I would provide potato salad to the working men for lunch."

Bracing herself for Henry's reaction, she kept her eyes on the Hahn farm as they drove by. Hope had planted daisies and marigolds in front of her large farmhouse. They turned on the road leading to their farm and passed the Weber house. Rose and Jeff had tied a tire to the limb of an elm tree in the front yard.

He chuckled. "I might be stubborn, but you seem to have the Almighty on your side this time. I won't go against Him, but don't expect me to become all chummy with the other men."

The tears she had held back now flowed freely.

He glanced over. "What did I say wrong now?"

"Nothing. I'm crying because I'm happy."

He shook his head. "I never will understand women."

Vivian smiled and scooted closer to him. If God would answer her prayer with something this impossible, maybe He did love her after all.

*****

As Henry parked near the school, Vivian wiped her brow. The heat had already become stifling when she woke early to prepare the potato salad. Now the stickiness clung to her dress.

At least women no longer felt compelled to wear cumbersome garments and corsets like they had a few years ago. Her mother and grandmother would sometimes suffer from heatstroke on a day like this.

It was a great era to be a woman. A couple of months ago, Congress had even passed an amendment to allow women the right to vote. Next year, for the first time, Vivian would be able to cast her vote for president of the United States. She still hadn't decided whether to do such a thing, but it was great to know she could if she wanted to. Maybe she should ask Henry what he thought about women voting.

Henry grabbed the potato salad, swept his other arm around her, and kissed her. All thoughts of politics left her mind. It lasted a little too long for being in public, and she thought about pulling away as she leaned into his embrace. The kiss stopped as abruptly as it started.

Heat warmed Vivian's cheeks, and she looked around to see it anyway was staring at them. It didn't look like anyway noticed, but she couldn't help the butterflies in her stomach. What would her mother have said if she were alive?

Henry headed to where the rest of the men gathered. She took the bowl to the food table.

Rose waddled over to her and patted her growing stomach. "Thank you for helping us today."

Mrs. Oster came over. "I never would have believed Henry would come here to lend a hand. You have done wonders with that man."

Vivian snatched a funeral fan from the table. "I didn't do a thing." *Except pray.* "Henry wanted to help. After all, our children will attend this school too."

"Are you telling us the stork is paying you a visit?" Mrs. Oster rubbed her hands together. "This is wonderful news. I can't wait to share it."

"No, wait." Vivian fanned harder. "I meant when the time comes."

Mrs. Oster raised an eyebrow. "It's been four months since you said your vows."

Vivian bit her lip. There was no way she would tell that nosy woman they'd only been living as husband and wife for a week.

Rose patted her hand. "Don't worry about it, dear. It took Jeff and me six months before I got in the family way. Now I don't seem to be able to stop."

"True," Mrs. Oster said. "Not every woman ends up like Hope." She turned to Rose. "Where is your sister today? I didn't see her at church yesterday. Is she ill?"

Rose's lips pressed together. "Mrs. Oster, I'll have you know Hope is on the nest. Has been for about four months now. Doctor Oster told her she should rest and not exert herself."

Mrs. Oster looked like her stomach had turned sour. "He didn't tell me anything about it."

"Maybe because my sister asked him to keep it quiet." Rose said. "With all the miscarriages she's had, I'm sure you can understand her decision to wait to make the announcement until her fourth month."

"Yes, of course." Mrs. Oster smile slipped. "Will you excuse me? I need a word with my husband."

As soon as she walked away, Vivian couldn't help but let out a chuckle.

"That woman sure gets out of sorts when the latest gossip is kept from her," Rose said.

"How is your sister doing?"

Rose's brow furrowed as she smoothed out her dress. "She's never carried a child to the fourth month before. Doctor Oster says it's a good sign. We're all praying. Hope would make such a good mother. She's wonderful with my children."

"I'm sure she'll be fine." Vivian let up a silent prayer for Hope.

Rose turned to the other women. "Ladies, we have two hours to spread this meal out. The men are going to be hungry, so let's get busy."

After helping lay out the meal, Vivian stood outside and watched to see how Henry was doing. Most of the men worked as a team on one side of the roof, but Henry nailed shingles on the other side alone. She'd be sure to remind him to try to be sociable when the men took their break.

When lunch was called, Henry waited until the rest of the men got in line before taking his place. After filling his plate with food, he came toward her. "How about we eat together?"

Vivian splayed her hand across her chest. "I assumed you'd eat with the men. I planned to eat with the women."

His face dropped.

"I guess it would be all right."

Henry walked toward an old maple tree where a blanket had been spread out. "We could sit here."

After they had their fill of fried chicken and potato salad, Vivian leaned against the tree. "I noticed you weren't working with the others."

"I work better by myself." He wiped a napkin across his mouth.

"Wouldn't it be better to help the other men?"

"I'm doing my part. What do you want from me?" Henry stood and strode toward the school building to collect his tools and get back to work.

When the other men saw him, they cut their lunch break short and headed toward the school. Henry approached the ladder with the tools he needed. Sheriff Abe darted toward him and started talking with him.

Vivian couldn't hear what they were saying, but one thing was sure. Whatever Abe said made Henry angry. He grabbed his tools and tramped toward her. "Vivian, get in the car. We're going home."

Chapter Eight

When they arrived home, Henry plopped onto his easy chair and let out a sigh. Vivian removed her hat but didn't say anything. He rolled his shoulders to try to get rid of the tightness.

She was quiet on the way home, but it was only a matter of time. Not only did he ruin her plans for him to become friends with the men of the community, he embarrassed her by storming off. He wouldn't blame her if she did nag him about it.

She sauntered behind his chair, and when he started to turn to see what she was up to, she massaged his shoulders.

He flinched, not because he didn't want her to continue, but because he was so startled by her kindness.

"You need to relax." She squeezed, kneading the tension away.

Henry leaned into her touch. "I'm sorry about what happened. I really did intend on working at the school all day."

"Shhh, it's all right. I know you did. When you're ready you can tell me what the sheriff said."

A knot formed in Henry's stomach. He moved away from her massaging hands and pulled her onto his lap.

Her gaze bored into him. "Whatever's eating you, I'm on your side. You know that, don't you?"

He wrapped his arms around her and kissed her. He didn't want to let go, but after a few moments, he pulled back. "It was my fault. I didn't want to work with the other men. Abe told me things would go faster if we shingled the roof together."

"What made you leave?" She raised an eyebrow. "He had to have said more."

Henry swallowed. "He had no right to order me around."

Her lips pressed together, and she pulled away. "I best get supper on. I didn't plan on us eating here." She headed to the kitchen.

"Wait." He blocked her path. "I know I shouldn't have left, but I can't abide Abe acting like the hero."

She blinked and for a moment, he was afraid the tears would

start up. "Henry, could you at least tell me what you have against Abe? There's more to it than what happened with me. He apologized and mended his ways year ago."

Henry nodded and followed Vivian to the sofa.

Vivian grabbed his hand. "Just say it. Why are you so angry with Abe?"

"Maybe it's not Abe I'm mad at. It was more my fault."

"What was your fault?" The warmth in her eyes almost made him feel like he could tell her the truth.

"I…I killed my mother."

*****

Vivian gasped as the air sucked out of the room. "How… Your mother died in childbirth. You didn't kill her. You're not making any sense."

His voice thickened. "I might as well have."

She forced her breathing to calm before saying any more. "Why don't you tell me why you think you killed your mother and what Abe has to do with this?"

Henry lowered his eyes and began to tell her the story in a monotone voice. "After Abe tried to force himself on you, he wouldn't let it drop. He was always after me to fight him. I wouldn't give him the satisfaction. It wasn't because I was scared of him, but I knew my father would blow up. He always told me to stay out of other people's business, and well, I couldn't let it go when Abe went after you. I just couldn't."

His hand trembled, and she clutched it to keep him steady. "One day, when he started talking bad about my mother, I fought him. His friends joined in, and he would have pounded me into the ground if James hadn't come out of nowhere to join my side."

She bit her bottom lip. James was like that, always coming to the aid of a friend. "So you fought. I still don't see what that has to do with your mother."

Henry cleared his throat, but he kept his gaze on his shoes. "When I got home, my father insisted on knowing what the fight was about. I told him everything. What choice did I have? He went into a rage about how he warned me not to get involved. He grabbed his razor strap and started whipping me with it."

"Oh, Henry, I'm so sorry. You suffered for helping me."

Henry glanced at her. "I would have done it again." His focus went back to his shoes. "I shouldn't have fought Abe. Anyway, I guess my mother had enough of his ways and shielded me with her body. He threw her off, and she landed on the fireplace hearth. The poker dug into her belly." His Adam's apple bulged. "She screamed out in pain. The doctor said she lost too much blood. My mom and my baby brother died that night, and it was my fault. Dad told everyone it was an accident, that she had lost her balance and fell, but I know the truth. If I'd held on to my temper when Abe was taunting me, my mother would still be alive."

Vivian touched his face, longing to comfort him. "It's not true. Don't you see? If anyone's responsible for your mother's death, it's your father? Your mother was trying to protect you."

The muscle in his cheek twitched. "No, if I'd done what he told me, she'd be alive. If Abe hadn't kept pushing it…"

Heat traveled up Vivian's back. She pulled her hand away. "If you'd done what your father told you, I might not have escaped that day." She turned to face him. "If you'd done what your father told you, your mother might have died anyway, but I'd be dead too."

Henry s gaze shot toward her. "Abe wouldn't have killed you."

"So, it would have been all right if he'd forced himself on me?"

He rubbed his hand over his face. "That's not what I meant. I'm glad I was there to help you."

"Henry." She took a deep breath and let it out before sitting back on the sofa beside him. "If you hadn't cared about me enough to come to the hotel to rescue me from Adder, I was planning to end it all by nightfall."

His forehead wrinkled as understanding crossed his features. "You planned to kill yourself?"

Vivian nodded as she wiped the tears strewn across her cheeks. "Didn't see I had anything left to live for. You brought hope back into my life. I'm so grateful you didn't do what your father always told you. You got involved in my life. You saved me."

He didn't say anything making her insides quiver. Maybe she shouldn't have told him. Would he withdraw from her? The ticking of the mantle clock slowed until her heart beat twice between every stroke as the hope Henry would forgive her pulsed away. Along with the hope God would forgive her.

He stood, stepped toward her, and swept her into his arms. "I didn't know." He kissed her passionately until she was lightheaded from his love. "I'll always be there to save you." He enveloped her until she felt safe in his arms. He leaned back and lifted her chin. "I promise I'll try to be a neighbor like the Good Samaritan, but I need time to change."

She pressed her lips together. "What about Sheriff Abe? He was just a kid when it happened. He reformed years ago. He's a different person now."

Henry pulled away. "Don't ask me to forgive Abe. I can't."

Chapter Nine

Vivian had a glow about her as Henry escorted her into the church for Christmas Eve service. Maybe the candlelight from the lit candelabra on the fireplace caused her face to beam. Or maybe it was because they were about to spend their first Christmas together.

Things had been better between them over the last few months. Ever since he told her about what happened to his mother and had promised to try to be a good neighbor, they'd been closer somehow. He couldn't believe someone like Vivian could love him, but she proved it to him every day since then.

He still hadn't been able to keep his promise to her although he started taking steps toward it. He would say hello to Jeff, Archie, and some of the other men when he saw them at the store or at church. He even asked Jeff about his newborn son and apologized for running out on them, but the opportunity to help them had never come up since that Saturday at the school.

Getting chummy with them was out of the question, but it didn't hurt to try to be a little friendlier and to help where needed if it made Vivian happy. As long as that didn't include becoming friends with Abe, he could handle being a good neighbor.

Jeff strode toward them. "Henry, could we talk?"

"Sure." Henry turned to Vivian. "Go ahead and find us a seat. I'll be there soon."

Vivian nodded and headed toward the pews in the front. Henry preferred a seat in the back where he wouldn't be noticed, but since his wife started getting closer to God, she insisted on sitting near the front, and he would follow her anywhere.

Jeff crossed his arms and scrunched his eyebrows together.

"Is something wrong?" Henry asked.

"Yes, Hope gave birth to a stillborn last night. She had a hard time of it, and the doc says it's unlikely she'll ever be able to have any more children."

Henry s stomach knotted. Even though he tried to keep to himself, he couldn't help but hope and pray Archie and Hope would have a healthy child this time. "I'm so sorry. Is there anything we can do to help?"

"As a matter of fact," Jeff rubbed his hand across his neck. "Rose has been staying with her sister, taking care of her, and well, tomorrow being Christmas, it would be nice if somebody could go over there and help Archie and Hope out. It would give Rose a chance to be with the kids and me a chance to see my wife and newborn son."

Henry raised an eyebrow. "Who did you have in mind?"

"You and Vivian. You don't have any children or family to spend Christmas with, and I figured Vivian could take care of Hope while you're there for Archie in case he wants to talk or something. He could use a friend right now."

Henry pulled at his bowtie. "I'm not good at that. Why didn't you ask Sheriff Abe and Nadine? Abe's closer to Archie than I am."

"Nadine's in the family way, and they were planning to go to Dayton to be with Abe's folks for Christmas. His dad had a stroke last year, and this might be his last Christmas."

"I don't know." As much as Henry wanted to prove he could be a good neighbor, he wasn't about to ruin his first Christmas with Vivian.

"I hate to ask, but my young'uns are having a tough time with this, and not having their mother home for Christmas…"

Henry loosened his collar. His tie was beginning to feel more like a noose. "I can't disappoint Vivian. This is our first Christmas together."

The muscle in Jeff's cheek twitched. "Of course. I wouldn't want to ruin your holiday for something so trivial. I'm sorry I troubled you."

As Jeff sauntered away, Henry's face flushed. His excuses did sound unimportant even to him after Archie and Hope had been through so much. He glanced at Vivian knowing this would disappoint her. As much as she'd been looking forward to their Christmas together, she would be angry if she knew what it had cost.

Henry swallowed, pulled off his tie, and marched to the pew where Jeff sat alone with eight of his children. "Vivian and I will be there first thing tomorrow morning."

*****

Vivian didn't say anything on the way home from church or as they sat by the fire in the living room. Something was bothering Henry, and she'd let him work it out before she pried. He had a habit of mulling over things before he talked to her. Sometimes it would be days before he'd come to her.

This time, she wouldn't let this go on until bedtime. Whatever was eating at him needed to be sorted out tonight. Nothing could be allowed to spoil the news she planned to tell him this Christmas.

She gazed at the pine tree. Henry thought it was silly to have a tree in the house, but when she told him how much she wanted one, he marched out into the snow and chopped down the fullest tree he could find. She'd spent the last week making a popcorn chain, sewing handmade ornaments, and making a quilted angel for the top. It wasn't fancy, but it was the nicest she'd ever had.

She remembered decorating trees and baking cookies with her mother when she was about six. Soon after, her father's started gambling and drinking and her family stopped celebrating Christmas, Easter, and birthdays. The holidays usually ended in arguments between her mother and father anyway.

This year would be different. Not only would she and Henry have their first Christmas together, but in seven months, they would celebrate the birth of their first child. Maybe it would be a boy. They could name it James. A sliver of sadness came over her. Thankfully, Henry understood her melancholy and shared her grief for his best friend.

"I have something to tell you." Henry's voice startled her. He was still staring at his coffee cup.

"I knew something was bothering you. Go ahead."

"It wasn't announced in church because the family wants some time before all the well-wishers come around, but Jeff told me Hope went into labor last night."

She almost blurted out what great news it was, but something was wrong. She could read it in Henry's face.

"The baby was stillborn."

Vivian struggled to find the air to breathe.

Henry took her hand. "She's all right, but the doctor says it was a hard birthing and she probably won't be able to have any children."

A tear fell down her cheek. "Oh Henry, I feel so bad for her. Did you tell Jeff we'll help however we can?"

"Yes, I told him." His Adam's apple bulged. "He wanted us to go over there tomorrow and help so Rose could spend the day with their children. I know you planned on us having breakfast in front of the tree and you having a fancy Christmas supper, and I tried to tell why we couldn't come…"

She held her breath.

"I hope you're not too disappointed, but we're spending our first Christmas at the Hahns."

Vivian practically bounced as she threw herself into Henry's arms. "I can't think of a better way to spend the holiday. I'll bring our dinner over there. They'll need to eat too. I have a ton of things to do before morning. I need to pack a basket with everything we'll need. Do you think I should make some cinnamon rolls for the morning? It would be easier than a large breakfast."

Henry stared at her with a strange look on his face. "I thought you would be angry."

"Why would you think that?"

He stroked his chin. "I ruined our first Christmas together."

"You didn't ruin it." She leaned against his chest listening to the beat of his heart. "You showed me how much you love me. Three months ago, you would have never agreed to this, and I would have spent Christmas tied up in knots worrying about Hope." She'd wait to tell him about their baby until they returned from the Hahn's tomorrow night. It would still be the best Christmas ever.

Something in Henry's eyes frightened her. He looked like a frightened boy who would do anything avoid this. She stroked his cheek with the back of her hand.

She wished she could find a way to reassure him.

Chapter Ten

Vivian let out a deep breath before entering Hope's room. After what she'd been through, Hope was sure to be as distraught as Vivian was when she contemplated ending her own life. Vivian didn't know how to comfort her. She pushed open the door.

Hope looked up and smiled. "Come in, Vivian. Thanks so much for coming."

Vivian sat in the chair next to the bed. "I'm happy to help."

"I told Rose we'd be fine, but she insisted on staying unless we could find someone to take her place. She's an old mother hen. You would think I was the younger sister."

Hope looked pale, but she seemed in good spirits, something Vivian wasn't expecting under the circumstances. "I brought food for Christmas dinner if you're up to it. How are you feeling?"

"I'm still a bit weak, but the doctor says that's to be expected. I lost a lot of blood, but I'll be fine in a couple of days. Christmas dinner sounds wonderful. He told me to make sure I eat good to keep up my strength."

Vivian swallowed. "I… I don't know what to say. I expected to find you distraught after what happened, but you seem to be… almost cheerful."

Hope's eyes closed and her head tilted back into the pillow. "I have my moments. Trust me." She opened her eyes and smiled. "I keep my hope in Jesus Christ, and He gives me the peace I need to get through this."

Vivian held back a snort. "How can you of all people talk of hope knowing you'll never have any children?"

Hope pressed her lips together as she propped herself up on her pillow. "If my hope rested on having children, then you're right. There would be no reason, but my hope is the kind they talk about in Psalms. 'But now, Lord, what do I look for? My hope is in you.'"

"I guess I don't understand that kind of hope. Henry reads the Bible every night. I'm trying to do what it says, but ever since James died…" She swallowed. "It's not that I don't love Henry. I do, but I expected to be spending my life with James."

Hope patted her hand. "You still miss him, don't you?"

"Yes." It came out as a whisper.

"Sometimes bad things happen. We'll probably never know why this side of Heaven, but we can trust God to work it out for the best. I don't know what God has planned, but I trust Him, so I have hope."

Vivian let out a chuckle. "I'm supposed to be cheering you up, not the other way around." She stood and headed for the door. "One thing I do know for certain, that Christmas dinner isn't going to cook itself, and I don't trust Archie or Henry to know the first thing about cooking a turkey."

*****

Henry slipped into the spare bedroom to keep Vivian from seeing him. He couldn't let her know he heard what she said.

I expected to be spending my life with James.

His eyes burned as he swallowed back the lump in his throat. He missed James too, but he thought she had grown to love him the same way she loved James. Now he knew the truth.

He wanted to make his excuses to Archie and leave her there. He needed to be alone to work this out. What difference did it make? Vivian needed him to take care of her, and he'd be there for her even if James would always come between them.

He made his way downstairs Why God didn't save James? He was the one who should have died.

Plunking onto the davenport next to Archie, he kneaded the back of his neck.

Archie hadn't said much since they got there, so they sat looking at the fire in the fireplace as a quietness hung between them. It should have been uncomfortable, but Henry was glad Archie wasn't in a talkative mood.

Soon Vivian came bouncing down the stairs on her way to the kitchen. "Archie, do you like cornbread? I thought I'd make it for supper."

Archie spoke in a low tone. "That's fine."

She swooped over to Henry and kissed him on the cheek. "I best get busy then. The turkey will be ready in an hour, and I don't even have the potatoes peeled yet."

The kiss felt warm on his cheek, but his stomach churned.

How many times had she kissed him, wishing it were James?

The rest of the day went pretty much the same way. Nobody said much of anything until Henry and Vivian got ready to leave.

"Thanks, Henry." Archie shook his hand. "I fretted you might spend the day trying to cheer me up or take my mind off what happened." He cleared his throat. "You were a true friend being there with me, allowing me to be quiet."

Henry nodded and walked out the door.

On the way home, Vivian chattered on about children and something Hope said about trusting God. Henry didn't hear most of it. What she said about not loving him the way she loved James kept flittering through his mind.

At the beginning of the day, he thought this might be the best Christmas he ever had, but he could see it now. He would never make her happy. Her happiness died with James.

He parked the car next to the house and escorted her in.

"I'll make us some coffee." Her voice had an unusual lilt about it.

Henry slumped in his chair by the fireplace. Maybe it would be better to let her know what he'd heard. If she didn't love him and never would, was it right to force her to stay in this marriage?

Vivian glided into the room and set the cup of hot coffee on the inn table next to the chair before sitting beside him. She gazed at him and took his hand in hers. "I have something to tell you."

A shiver went through him. This was it. She was going to tell him she was leaving. He let out the breath he was holding. Better to get it over with. "Go on."

Vivian said something he couldn't make out and grinned so wide it was amazing her face contained the smile.

Henry sat still not knowing what to say or do. He felt like he was in a trench somewhere in Germany with bombs overhead. The words she said didn't register.

"Did you hear me, Henry? I'm on the nest."

As what she said bored its way inside his heart, a relief washed over him. He stood and took her in his arms. "You're not leaving me?" He held her tight. She was the rope holding him as he dangled over a steep ravine.

"No, silly." She pulled back. "Of course I'm not leaving you. Whatever gave you that idea? I'm going to have your baby in about seven months. I love you."

Warmth filled his chest. "I love you too." He picked her up and carried her into the bedroom. Now with a baby on the way, he felt like a condemned man who had just heard from the governor he'd been pardoned. He would do whatever he had to do to make her love him like she did James. Whatever it took.

Chapter Eleven

Vivian's face looked flushed as she burst into the living room. It had been two months since she'd announced she was pregnant, and she was just beginning to show. "Henry, have you ever had chicken pox?"

"Yes," Henry set down her newspaper. "Why?"

"I've never had them before now." She lifted her blouse to show a blistery rash on her stomach. Her eyes watered. "Do you think it will hurt the baby?"

"Of course not." He tried to force a reassuring smile. "Everyone gets chicken pox at some point in their life, but just to make sure, I'll get Doctor Oster. Why don't you lie down?"

After getting into her nightgown and climbing into bed, Vivian started coughing.

Henry skirted to her bedside. "Are you all right?"

"Yes." She coughed some more. "It's silly to get the doctor. Like you said, everyone gets chicken pox."

He kissed her forehead. She was burning up with fever. "I'm not taking any chances with you or the baby. Do you think you'll be all right while I fetch him? I could go to the Weber farm and get Rose to stay with you."

"I'll be fine." Vivian closed her eyes. "I just want to rest a little."

"I'll be as quick as I can." Henry darted toward the door. "And don't scratch. You're too beautiful to have chicken pox scars."

She chuckled as he left.

On the drive into town, he tried to convince himself there was nothing to worry about. He made it to Doctor Oster's office in twenty minutes and mucked through the mud to the front door.

All the rain they'd been having reminded him of the trenches he and James lived in during the war. The sludge seeped into every ounce of the clothing and only washed off during the torrential rainfalls flooding their dugouts. James used to joke they were better equipped to handle the conditions since they lived in Ohio most of the lives.

At least the sun was finally shining. They needed a few sunny days to dry out the land.

He knocked on the door.

Mrs. Oster answered. "What is it? You like to have pounded my door down."

Henry swallowed. "Is Doctor Oster here?"

"No, he's out making house calls. One of the Weber boys broke his leg. Then there's Widow Hoffman. She's been feeling poorly lately, probably her rheumatism acting up with all the rain we've been having. Sheriff Abe wanted him to stop by. There's a prisoner there who has the chicken pox if you can believe that. A grown man getting the chicken pox."

Henry rubbed his temple.

"Oh dear," Mrs. Oster said. "Do you have a headache? I know where my husband keeps his headache powders. You don't need to call on him for a little headache, you know. He's a busy man."

After closing his eyes for a moment to keep from making a snide remark, Henry interrupted her. "Could you have him stop by when he gets back?"

Mrs. Oster raised an eyebrow. "Why? Is something wrong with Vivian? I heard she's in the family way."

Henry pressed his lips together. "Just have him stop by. Tell him it's important." He tipped his hat and hurried home to Vivian.

When he got back, he sat by the bed and put his hand on her forehead. She was even hotter than before. "Would you like a cup of tea?"

"That would be nice." She touched Henry's hand. "Thank you."

He stroked her hair. "I'll be right back." He went to the kitchen and set the tea kettle on the stove. *Lord, please let her be all right.*

When he managed to get the tea made, he took it to her bedside, but she'd fallen asleep. He covered her with the extra quilt and sat in the rocker by the bed watching her. Maybe being there could somehow make her well.

He was worrying about nothing. After all, it was chicken pox, not the influenza that killed over fifty million people a couple of years ago. It was the chicken pox.

Henry startled to the sound of knocking. It had been early

afternoon when he brought the tea, and now it was already dusk.

He answered the door and ushered Doctor Oster to the bedroom where Vivian was still sleeping. "She has the chicken pox. I know it was silly to bother you about it, but she's burning up and with her being in the family way..."

Doctor Oster opened his medical bag and pulled out a thermometer. "You were right to call me, son. In adults, especially pregnant women, chicken pox can lead to complications."

The muscle in Henry's jaw twitched. "Is she going to be all right? What about the baby?"

The doctor patted his arm. "Don't worry so much. She's in her fourth month, so she should be fine." He placed a hand on Henry's back and directed him toward the door. "Now you need to leave so I can examine my patient."

Henry obeyed the doctor and sauntered into the living room, but his footsteps felt sluggish like bricks were tied to his shoes. He slunk into his chair and tried to focus on the newspaper article about the twenty-nine radical anarchists who were being held in New Jersey. A secret service agent said they were the worst terrorists ever captured on American soil.

He set the paper down and started pacing. What was taking so long?

The door opened, and Doctor Oster motioned Henry back into the room. "I've finished my examination, and your wife has a typical case of the chicken pox."

Vivian sat up in the bed coughing. When it subsided, she sunk into her pillow. "I told you there was no reason to fret."

Doctor Oster crossed his arms. "Henry has every reason to worry. Chicken pox in an adult can be serious."

Henry grabbed hold of her hand. "Will she be all right?"

"Probably." The doctor put his supplies back in his black bag. "Do you have a thermometer?"

"No, never saw the sense of it. I know how sick I am by how I feel. I don't need some thing-a-ma-jig to tell me."

Doctor Oster handed him a thermometer. "Well, you need one now. Her temperature is a hundred and three degrees. It should be ninety-eight point six. Take it every couple of hours by placing it under her tongue for three minutes. If it gets to a hundred and four or doesn't go down within a couple of days, or if it hurts for her to breathe, you come fetch me."

Henry rubbed his hand over his face. "Will she be all right or not?" He said it with a bit more edge than usual.

The doctor hesitated and gave Henry a probing gaze. When he did speak, his words were a smooth as freshly churned butter. "She should be fine as long as her temperature lowers within a couple of days. If this develops into chicken pox pneumonia... Just let me know if she gets worse."

"Thank you, doctor," Vivian said, then closed her eyes. The blisters already splotched across her face.

As they made their way outside, Doctor Oster gave Henry instructions on how to care for Vivian. "I'll be back in a few days to check on her. You just do as I said, and don't fret so much. Most often, it'll run its course. She'll be up and around cooking your meals before you know it."

"Thank you, Doctor."

Oster paused before opening his car door. "Do you want me to stop by the Hahn's and ask Hope to help? I'm sure she wouldn't mind."

Henry pressed his lips together. He sure didn't want anyone else meddling when he was so worried about his wife. "No need."

"Suit yourself," Doctor Oster said. "I'll be back in a few days to check on her."

Henry nodded. After Doctor Oster left, he strode to the bedroom and sat in the rocking chair. Vivian had fallen asleep. Maybe that was a good thing. Resting would help her get better. He cupped his hands over his mouth and nose. *Please, Lord. I need her.*

*****

It had been two days, and Vivian still had a high fever. Only now, she couldn't get any rest because of the constant coughing.

Henry brought the thermometer to the window and read the gauge. 103.9. He couldn't wait any longer. He needed to get Doctor Oster here, but how could he leave her like this?

He stroked her hair. "Vivian."

She gave him a glassy stare. The pox had covered her face and surrounded her mouth and eyes. She even had some on her tongue.

"I'm going to get the doctor. I'll only be gone twenty minutes."

She didn't say anything.

After pulling the blanket up to her chin, he rushed outside and cranked the automobile. The rain pelted his back drenching his coat, but he didn't pay it any mind. All that mattered was Vivian. He drove through some ruts as water splashed the windows of the car. As he passed the Weber's farm, he considered stopping for a moment to ask Rose to sit with Vivian, but it would take too much time. The sooner he got to the doctor's office, the quicker he'd be back.

After parking in front of the office, Henry pounded on the door almost as hard as his heart pounded in his chest. Nobody answered. He hurried next door and knocked on the door of Doctor Oster house.

He has to be there. Please don't let his wife answer.

Mrs. Oster opened the door. "Henry, what are you doing out in this storm?"

Thunder rumbled to emphasize her point.

"I need Doctor Oster." Henry tried to keep the panic out of his voice. "Vivian's worse."

"Well, come in here out of the rain." Mrs. Oster opened the door wider. "With all these storms we've been having, it reminds me of when the Ohio River flooded about this time near on two years ago."

Henry stepped into the foyer but would go any further. "Mrs. Oster, please. I left her alone. I need the doctor."

"You left her alone?" The tone of her voice accused him. "Why didn't you get Rose or Hope to stay with her?"

"Mrs. Oster, please." He hated the pleading in his voice. If only she would hurry, just this once.

She tilted her chin. "I'll get him."

Doctor Oster strode to the entrance a moment later and grabbed his black bag off the foyer table. "Let's go."

Henry let out a breath as they rushed to the car. Lightening lit up the hazy sky. He got behind the wheel and drove home faster than he thought the Model T could go.

When they reached Archie Hahn's farm, Doctor Oster ordered, "Stop here."

Henry pulled up to the farmhouse. "Why? We have to get back to Vivian."

"You'll need Hope's help until Vivian's up on her feet."

Henry stared at the clutch. "I've been doing fine on my own."

Doctor Oster opened the door of the car and placed his coat over his head. "This isn't for you. Consider what Vivian needs."

Henry nodded.

The doctor ran toward the house.

The thickness in Henry's throat threatened to choke him. They'd already wasted enough time. *Please, hurry.* Vivian was alone. He should have stopped to have Rose look in on her. Thunder crashed, and then lightning lit up the sky.

A moment later, Doctor Oster rushed to the car and got inside. "Archie and Hope will meet us at the house."

"Archie's coming too?" Henry shifted the car into gear and drove toward home. "Why?"

"He insisted. Said you were there for him when Hope lost the baby, and he'd like to return the favor."

Henry jutted his jaw, turned the knob to flip the wipers, and stepped harder on the gas pedal. Whenever he needed to shift gears, he would have to let go of the wiper knob and allow the water to pour over the windshield until he couldn't see the road.

"Here, son," Doctor Oster reached for the knob. "I'll do that."

"I don't need your help." Henry gripped the wheel tighter. "Why can't everyone leave us be?"

The doctor ignored him, grabbed the knob, and operated the wipers.

Heat rushed to Henry's face and ears until he longed to open the window to let the rain cool him. When he drove up to his house, he didn't wait for Doctor Oster. He rushed inside leaving the front door open and dashed to the bedroom.

Vivian lay on the floor in a puddle of blood.

Chapter Twelve

Henry sat with shoulders slumped on the steps of the front porch almost numb with grief. Archie stayed at his side but didn't talk. He wanted to be left alone, but at the same time, he was grateful for the man's presence. At least, Archie didn't feel the need to say anything.

Doctor Oster's blue eyes had held such compassion when he'd told Henry Vivian had lost the baby. The chicken pox had turned into pneumonia, and she'd been alone when the miscarriage happened. Alone because he refused to stop and ask a neighbor for help.

Now he might lose his wife too.

"Prepare for the worst," Doctor Oster had said. "I might not be able to save her."

One rain storm after another had blown in since then. Finally, this morning, the rain stopped, and the sun began to peek through the clouds.

Knowing there was nothing he could do, he went outside, plopped on the porch steps not caring if they were still wet.

Archie finally spoke. "I'd like to pray with you."

Henry nodded, afraid if he voiced his consent, he might break down.

Archie laid a hand on his shoulder. "Lord we ask you to heal Vivian and for Henry to be comforted through this trying time. Amen."

Henry uttered his own prayer. "Please, Lord. Don't take her from me."

A sliver of light glimmered through the clouds creating a full double rainbow in the sky. Henry wiped his eyes and looked again. He had never seen a rainbow so vibrant, let alone a double rainbow. The rainbow was a promise in the Bible. Maybe this was God's way of telling him Vivian would be okay.

Doctor Oster came onto the porch. Henry stood and braced himself, but nothing would prepare him if this was bad news.

"The worst is over. She's going to be fine."

Henry's knees gave way. It was his fault the baby was dead, but he hadn't lost Vivian. He had another chance to protect her.

He would never allow harm to come to her again if he could help it. His mother had died in childbirth, but that wouldn't happen to Vivian. He would keep her safe by keeping his distance.

*****

Vivian ran to her room and slammed the door. It had been a month since she lost the baby, and Henry hadn't said more than two words to her. He'd retreated back into that shell of his and was more elusive than when he married her. It was obvious he blamed her for what happened.

When she came down sick, he'd moved back into his old room. Tonight, she had cooked him his favorite meal and suggested he move back into their bedroom. She touched his cheek with her hand.

He brushed her hand away. "No need. We both get more sleep with me upstairs."

"Who said I wanted to sleep?"

Henry didn't say a word. He just grabbed that newspaper of his and hid behind it. She snatched it from him, threw it in the fireplace, and stormed into her room.

Tears poured down her face. Hope had told her how he collapsed when he found out she'd be all right. There had to be some passion deep inside him somewhere.

She'd managed to get him to show affection before, but how could she crack that shell again? She sat at her writing desk and started a list. Their anniversary was a couple of months away. She didn't want to wait that long, but Palm Sunday was in only four weeks.

He'd come to her rescue last year on Palm Sunday. She would make that her deadline. She blew her nose. Had it been almost a year since he'd marched into that hotel and asked her to marry him? It seemed longer and shorter at the same time.

She tapped her pencil on the desk. Henry seemed to respond a few months back when she made the navy-blue dress she wore to Nadine's wedding. She wrote *make new dress* on the list.

Resting her pencil on her chin, she remembered the date in Greenville with them consummating their marriage. He'd told her she'd look cute as a flapper. She wrote *knit a cloche hat, string beads for a necklace,* and *cut hair* on the list.

She still needed to cook his favorite meal. She would dawn her new look and fix fried chicken for Sunday dinner. She was sure she had enough time get everything done, especially since Henry didn't pay much attention to her lately.

He wouldn't even see it coming. She'd make the day so special he couldn't resist falling for her again.

A lump formed in her throat. What if Henry had never really loved her? After all, her own father didn't even care about her. All he loved was his gambling.

Wiping her eyes, she uttered a prayer. This had to work. She had to find a way to make Henry adore her as much as she adored him.

The last thing she wrote on the list was to act sweet no matter how much he provoked her. She'd do what he wanted and stay away from the neighbors. She would become the type of woman he could love.

She bit her bottom lip. *This has to work.*

*****

Henry stayed in the barn taking care of the animals longer than he needed. His life had become a series of moves to avoid Vivian.

It wasn't unpleasant to be around her. Quite the opposite. No matter how much he tried to distance her, she had been so sweet lately that his passion for her was hard to resist. He couldn't give in. He loved her too much to risk her life by making her pregnant again, especially since she would never love and respect him the way she did James.

Vivian stepped out on the porch. "Breakfast is ready."

He grabbed the milk pail. There was no dodging it any longer. He sauntered into the house and sat at the kitchen table, a condemned man eating his last meal.

He focused on his plate filled with scrambled eggs, bacon, and toast. Vivian was a fine cook. There was some kind of spice she used in the eggs. Whatever it was, her scrambled eggs were the best he s ever eaten.

While grabbing his coffee mug, he risked a glance at her. She gazed at him with those big brown doe eyes of hers. When she looked at him like that, it took everything inside him to resist her. He took a sip and diverted his eyes to the eggs as he ate another bite.

"Next week is Palm Sunday." She had a lilt in her voice.

"Yep," he said between bites.

"Do you remember last Palm Sunday?"

He squeezed his napkin and wiped the corners of his mouth, but he didn't dare look at her again. "I remember."

"I was so grateful when you showed up like one of those knights in shining armor, like out of one of those storybooks."

Clutching his napkin between his fingers, he glanced at her. She simpered. A piece of egg had attached itself to the corner of her mouth. Her eyes gazed so longingly trying to draw him into surrendering. "I only did it because I promised James to look out for you."

The color drained from Vivian's face. She dropped her napkin, ran to her bedroom, and slammed the door.

Heat rose to his face. Maybe he should go to her, try to comfort her. He could tell her he didn't mean it, that he rescued her for his own sake -- because he adored her. Rushing to the bedroom door, he listened from the other side. The humming of a sewing machine was interrupted by a hiccup and occasional sob.

He placed his hand on the doorknob, then drew it back and walked away. If he went to her, he'd end up giving into his desires and hurting her more. Best to leave her alone.

Chapter Thirteen

Palm Sunday, 1920

As soon as Henry went outside to do his morning chores, Vivian rushed to the bedroom so she could accomplish the next thing on her list. Grabbing a pair of sewing shears, she looked in the mirror at her long auburn locks and paused.

Once she did this, there was no going back.

She bit her lip and put the scissors up to the long ringlet on the right side of her face. Exhaling a deep breath, she cut it off. That wasn't so bad. She cut off the next ringlet, and the next until her hair was bobbed.

Hair was flying up in different places, and she couldn't really tell what the final result was, so she grabbed a hair brush, wet it, and brushed through her short hair.

She stared at her reflection. Not bad. In fact, it looked pretty good. She wasn't sure she would have the nerve to wear it this short, but it looked chic, like it did in the moving picture she saw with Henry..

She grabbed a broom and swept the long curls strewn all over the floor into a dustpan and wrapped them in some butcher paper before throwing them away. She didn't want her husband to see them and suspect before she could spring the new flapper look on him.

After hurrying to get dressed before he came back, Vivian grabbed some long beads she'd borrowed from Nadene and wrapped them around her neck.

She examined herself in the full-length, oval mirror in the corner of her bedroom and smiled, pleased with the way the new, teal blue, lowered waist dress she'd sewn from the McCall Magazine pattern turned out. The hemline was a little shorter than she was used to, but she'd seen women wear shorter skirts to church. Nadine's dresses had to be at least an inch shorter. With her bobbed hair and long beads, she really did look like a flapper.

Please, Lord, let Henry notice.

She stepped into the kitchen to start breakfast. On Sunday

mornings, they usually had a light breakfast with rolls she made the night before and her homemade preserves. She placed the rolls in the oven to heat.

The door banged shut behind her. She twirled around to face Henry. His widened eyes and dropped chin made her chuckle. That was the reaction she'd hoped for. "So, what do you think?"

He sank into the kitchen chair. "You cut your hair."

She ran her fingers through it. "Do you like it?"

"I suppose it's all right."

She clamped her mouth shut. *All right! All right!* She took a slow steady breath to keep from saying something she'd regret. She promised herself she'd be super sweet today no matter what Henry said.

Besides, his reaction when he stepped through the door showed she was getting to him. She just needed to keep her temper until she prepared him a dinner fit for a king later this afternoon.

Nadine had told her the way to a man's heart was through his stomach. Maybe that was true. Henry usually ate her meals like he was starving to death.

After breakfast dishes were done, she tucked her hair in her new pink knitted cloche hat and slipped on her spring coat. Henry would come around. This had to work.

*****

Henry picked at his fried chicken. It was the best Vivian had ever made, but he couldn't get his mind off of her new appearance. Every time she looked away, he couldn't stop himself from catching another glance at her. She was always a beauty, but now... His heart beat faster. She had become a real Sheba.

All he wanted to do was wrap her in his arms, kiss her, and tell her how much he adored her. Instead, he cleared his throat, focused his eyes on his chicken leg, and ate another bite of mashed potatoes.

What made it worse was how she kept prattling on about how she'd sewn the dress from a pattern she'd found in McCall Magazine. "Everyone at church loved my new look. Rose loved the dress, and don't you just love my new cloche hat? I knitted it myself. Nadine said it was the bee's knees."

He grunted. "Where'd you get the beads?"

"I borrowed them from Nadine."

"Don't know if I like my wife borrowing from the neighbors." Especially not Abe's wife.

"I'll give them back tomorrow."

"See that you do." He wasn't really angry at her, but he tried to hold onto his ire to keep himself from touching her, kissing her.

She rattled on as if she didn't care what he thought about her borrowing those beads. "I cut my hair in the same style Mary Pickford wore hers in that movie we watched. You remember the one, *Daddy Longlegs*. I like it this way. It's not so heavy. I wanted to look nice for you and make this day special. I know it's not our anniversary or anything, but since you showed up at the Greenville Hotel last Palm Sunday..." She bit her bottom lip.

He almost reached out and touched her hand. He clenched his jaw. "Like you said, it's not our anniversary. You look fine, but don't you think your dress is a little... short? I'm not sure I like my wife parading around in bobbed hair and short skirts. It's not decent. Next, you'll be rolling down your hose, smoking, and going to speakeasies."

Vivian glower at him, her bottom lip trembling. He'd seen that look before, after the miscarriage. She blamed him for leaving her alone when she lost the baby. The storm clouds in her eyes were more threatening than any deadly tempest.

Moisture filled her eyes. "James would have liked my dress. He loved me." She ran out of the room.

All the air sucked out of him, and for a moment, he couldn't breathe. He should have been relieved. It was finally out in the open. Vivian wished James were alive so she wouldn't be stuck with him.

James would have said all the right words. James would have told her how pretty she was. She did look adorable with her new outfit and haircut, but Henry couldn't risk saying it. It was time to end this charade.

He would wait until after church to tell her he was leaving for Greenville in the morning. He was sure he could find a job there. He would hire a farm worker to help her. That way, she'd always have a place to live, and she could divorce him for abandonment.

It would be best for both of them. That glare she'd been given him said it all. She didn't love or respect him.

She'd be better off without him.

*****

Vivian washed the tears from her face. She didn't mean to say that about James. Besides putting Henry in a foul mood, it wasn't fair to him. She loved him every bit as much as she had loved James.

All she wanted was for her husband to show a little love and affection. Was that too much to ask? It wouldn't be if he really loved her.

It was time she faced the truth. God had deserted her again, and Henry would never love her the way James did.

Compliments had poured out of James like water flowing through the Great Miami River, but Henry restrained himself like the Englewood Dam held back the flood waters. He rarely said five words not involving raising pigs or growing corn.

Nothing she did or said matter to him. She'd even stopped going to sewing bees since the miscarriage because that's what he wanted, but no matter how hard she tried, she couldn't please him. Didn't he understand the dress and the haircut he disdained were for him?

She stepped into the drafty parlor she'd spent all her spare time decorating. Since she'd married Henry, she'd stripped the dingy yellow-flowered wallpaper and painted them a light blue. She'd sewn slipcovers for the old stained sofa and chair and made cushions for the rocker trying to make the room look like one of those parlors in Good Housekeeping.

Henry had kicked up the corner of the green rug covering the wooden floor and had knocked aside the doily on his overstuffed chair – the one she wanted to throw out, but he insisted on keeping it. He never cared about what she wanted.

She straightened the rug and doily. "I work hard to keep a tidy house. The least you could do is clean up after yourself. You don't care about anything I do around here."

He stiffened and walked outside.

Fine. Let him walk out on her.

She made sure everything was in place in the kitchen although she didn't know why she bothered, then she rushed out the front door to the road where their Model-T Ford sat. Dark clouds lingered overhead, and heaviness saturated the air displaying the dissension between them.

He stood by the car door, tall and gangly like one of his cornstalks, gazing at her with those empty dark eyes of his. His square jaw and stoic stance didn't show any emotion. He wasn't even distressed that she'd blurted out those ugly words earlier. He couldn't even stir up enough passion to be angry. "We're late."

"Sorry," was all Vivian could muster as she scooted into the front passenger seat. "Maybe we shouldn't go tonight. It looks like a bad storm is coming."

"It'll be all right." Henry cranked the starter, climbed in the driver seat to start the engine, and headed toward Resurrection of Hope Church for the evening service.

"You never listen to me." The tone she used made her cringe. It was the same way her mother talked to her father, but she couldn't help it. "It seems like the only reason I say anything is to hear my own voice." All the hurt she'd felt rose to the surface, and she couldn't tamp it down.

They drove along the dirt road where fields waited to be plowed. Near each field, a farmhouse and barn stood sentry, but it couldn't keep the storms from raging through. The wind whistled through the oak and ash trees shading the houses, blowing off some of the white buds making them look like snowflakes on the green lawns.

Droplets of rain hit the windshield. Henry moved the handle back and forth to operate the windshield wiper.

A wall of dark greenish clouds ahead made the sky look ominous. She tightened her grip on the armrest. "I'm telling you we should turn back."

"Just a spring storm. The land could use it."

Something in her had to try one more time. "I'm sorry for what I said about James." She swallowed. "I didn't mean it."

His jaw twitched. "Don't matter. Best we leave it alone."

She blinked to keep tears from being shed. It did matter, at least to her, even if he didn't love her enough to care. "Still, I had no right to say what I did."

Thunder rumbled in the distance, rolling in until it landed with a boom. Henry gazed in the direction of the noise. "I knew you didn't love me when I married you."

She shot him a look but didn't say any more. Just once, she

wished he would show some passion, jealousy, anger, fervor. If only he could love her as much as she loved him.

Sheet lightening lit up the sky as rain pelted the car windows. Crashes of thunder grew more frequent. Soon, the trees swaying under the weight of the deluge grew into blurs of grey, reflecting the bleakness of her marriage, until all she could see was the rain.

Henry slowed the Model-T to a crawl and grinded the lever to the wipers back and forth.

Lightning struck the sugar maple tree ahead of them, and it burst into flames as the green flowers spouted into the air. Vivian's stomach tightened. "Please, let's go back."

"The church is just a little further." Henry's calm tone never rattled. "Best we go on."

Torrents struck the car. Vivian held her breath.

They'd been through many storms before. They were a common occurrence to anyone living in Ohio, but this one seemed different. The weather echoed the fury in her soul.

*****

Henry swallowed the lump in his throat. He'd never seen a storm like this before. His mother once told him about the twister she survived as a little girl. Torrential rain, dark gray-green clouds, hail, and then a calm before it hit like a freight train. He had to keep going until they got to safety, and they were closer to the church than to the house. Out here in the middle of nowhere, he couldn't keep Vivian safe.

Pressing harder on the gas, he prayed he was going the right direction. He couldn't see clearly enough to know for sure, but he wouldn't let her down like he had his mother.

The Model-T jerked and bumped. He couldn't see the road in front of him, and he suspected he may have left the path, but the only thing he could do was keep going. The car hit a rut, and the front passenger side tilted forward. He stomped on the gas. The grinding of the tire spinning and the smell of rubber churned his stomach, but the car didn't move.

"Stay here." He pushed the car door open and stepped out into the storm.

Raindrops assailed his skin. Mortars of water bombarded him. He guarded his face with his jacket and felt along the side of his car until he could see the problem. The right front tire was in a ditch.

He wiped a hand over his face. He had to get the automobile out of the ditch. There were no houses around here, and they couldn't walk to the church in this storm. Scurrying back to the car, he got in, closed the door, and raised his voice to be heard over the rain. "We're stuck."

She gave him that same look of disgust she had earlier when she'd mentioned James earlier. "I told you we should have turned around. What are we going to do now?"

"Get behind the wheel. When I tell you, turn it hard to the left. I'll try to push it out."

Vivian swiped her tongue across her lips. "Maybe we should just wait until the storm dies down. Then we could walk to the church and get help."

He gazed at the sky and chewed on the inside of his cheek. The barricade of dark clouds had formed a swirling pattern. "No, we can't chance it."

"Why not? Why don't you ever listen to me?"

Henry worked his jaw back and forth. "Vivian, we can't stay here. This is twister weather."

She let out a gasp.

He opened the car door and got out. "Roll down the window so you can hear me."

She paused for a moment then scooted behind the steering wheel. He closed the door and headed to the back of the car as she cranked down the window. He braced his foot in the mud and tried to get a good stance as he leaned his shoulder against the car.

"All right. Foot off the brake. Turn the wheel." As he leaned into the car with all his might, the wheel turned. It inched forward but not enough. His foot slipped in the mud, and he struggled to brace it against something. The car rolled back. He jumped to get out of the way as the Model-T slid further into the ditch.

He locked around trying to find a tree limb or rock he could use to give him something solid to stand on as he pushed. A branch from the maple tree was a few feet away, but before he could get to it, something hard hit him on the forehead.

Hail the size of rocks pelted him. He pulled his coat over his head and ran back to the car. Struggling against the wind to pull the door open, he shouted, "Scoot over," and jumped inside, away from the ice pellets assaulting him.

Vivian touched his forehead with her handkerchief. "It's bleeding."

Henry brushed her hand away. "Listen. When the hail stops, we need to get away from here. Get to the church."

"Are you crazy? We can't go out in that. We need to stay in the car where it's safe."

"Vivian, we have to go." His heartbeats rivaled the throbbing of raindrops. "The water in the ditch is rising. We have maybe ten minutes before it tips the car over."

"Maybe we could take shelter under that grove of trees." She pointed to a clump of willow trees across the field.

He could hear the hitch in her voice and wanted to give in, but his desire to keep her safe won out. "We can't stay here. It's too dangerous. The church is only a half mile away."

Her lips pursed as she shot him that look. "I told you we shouldn't go tonight."

He kneaded the back of his neck but didn't answer. She was right. If he had turned back, they wouldn't be stuck out here. He'd failed her -- again.

A hailstone the size of a baseball shattered the glass on the front windshield. Vivian jumped.

Henry's jaw tightened. "We'll wait until the hail calms down."

The hail stones diminished in size then ceased, and the rain slowed to a drizzle like somebody had turned off the faucet on a sink in one of those fancy city houses with running water.

"We have to go now." He got out of the car and reached his hand toward hers. "Come on."

Vivian scooted out. He grasped her hand as they ran in the direction of the church.

He wanted to believe the storm was over, but he remembered how his mother had described the day that changed her life

"The rain and hail stopped," his mom had said as she wiped her eyes. "An eerie calm fell then the sound of a freight train, and the tornado snatched my papa off the face of the earth. I never saw him alive again. They didn't find his body 'til weeks later."

They had to get to the church soon. There was shelter there. As they ran, he grasped her hand tighter and pulled her along. The wind beat against their faces. A roaring sound caused Henry's chest to pound.

Vivian pointed up. "A twister!"

He barely had time to turn before the massive, gray, swirling funnel raced toward them. A tree limb blew past him, and he stepped back to avoid it.

"Over there!" He yelled, pointing to a ravine, but the wind caught his voice. He pushed Vivian to the ground and threw himself over her.

The wind pick her up for he landed. He reached for her hand and managed to grasp it, but he couldn't hold on. She slipped away. The tornado dissolved as quickly as it had swept in.

Henry beat his fists on the muddy ground.

Chapter Fourteen

Henry didn't know how long he lay there, but when he pulled himself to his feet, he had no more tears to cry. This was his fault. How could he have let go of her? He should have held on tighter. He shouldn't have taken her out. He know a bad storm was brewing. He should have protected her. The tornado swept through, and Vivian was gone.

His gaze darted across the landscape. Willow, oak, maple, and pine trees had been snapped in two. Limbs, rocks, and leaves littered the ground. His Model-T sat in the ditch where he'd left it. The tornado hadn't touched it. If only he'd listened to her. They would have been safe in the car.

The tears started flowing again as he sat in the mud. He wasn't sure he would ever leave this spot for the rest of his life.

He turned his face toward Heaven. "First my mother. Then James and the baby. Now Vivian. Why can't you take me? Why can't you just take me." His throat ached from the sobs. He couldn't go on without her.

The rain saturated every part of Henry's clothes and body as the sun hung low in the sky shielded by the dark clouds. He shivered but didn't bother to move from the mud where he sat. Let the sun go down. It gave no warmth or light since the storm hit anyway.

He looked up toward Heaven. "Lord, why didn't you let me die with her? Why couldn't you let me die on the battlefield?" James and Vivian could have been alive and together. At least they were together now.

A double bow spanned across the sky. Henry gasped. It was a promise like the last time he'd seen it. He couldn't have heard it clearer if God had spoken to him audibly. Somewhere out there, Vivian was alive.

He stood and peered the distance looking for signs in the debris littering the landscape. He would find her if he had to move Heaven and Earth to do it.

The rainbow faded, and sunset lit the western sky with red

and yellow.

Since the tornado came from the west, Henry set out toward the east. He would pace thirty or forty feet in each direction before going to the next section. It might take hours to get to the church and would be well after dark when he arrived, but it was the only way he could think of to find her.

He'd already lost time sitting in the mud feeling sorry for himself. This time, he wouldn't let Vivian down. If he found her dead, he'd deal with it when it came. In the meantime, he wouldn't stop looking.

The sun disappeared over the horizon, and with no moon or stars illuminating the sky, a murkiness set over the fields. He ran toward the Model-T thanking God he'd thought to keep a tungsten flashlight in the glove box.

He pulled open the door, grabbed it, and turning it on. Scanning the area, he paced thirty feet in each direction. It didn't give much light, but it would have to do. Not finding anything but broken tree limbs, his feet slushed in the muddy ground as he trudged another fifty feet and started the process again.

The rain started up again. Panic rose inside threatening to choke him. The words from a hymn came to mind, and he started singing.

"When peace, like a river, attendeth my way, When sorrows like sea billows roll; Whatever my lot, Thou hast taught me to say…" His voice choked up. *"It is well, it is well with my soul."*

*****

Vivian stirred but felt trapped. She couldn't move her legs. She kept her eyes closed for a moment. It was cold and wet. She felt numb. She didn't know where she was. "What happened?"

Henry had yelled at her to get down. He pushed her to the ground. He grabbed hold of her hand as the wind picked her up. The tornado.

A wave of nausea hit her. She groaned and squinted her eyes open. It was dark. The sun hadn't gone down yet when the tornado hit, and now it was well into the night, and it was still raining.

As her eyes adjusted, she looked around. She was head first in a gully, and a tree branch rested across her legs. At least she hoped her legs were there. She couldn't see or feel them.

84

She tried to sit up but couldn't. Letting out a groan, she pushed on the branch, but it wouldn't move.

How far was she from the road? "Help! Help!" Henry would hear her. "Help!" He would find her in time. She remembered the argument. If he bothered to look.

She shivered. It was so cold. If only she had a blanket or something to protect her from the cold. Her spring coat was drenched and weighted down with moisture.

Her dress. Her beautiful dress. It was covered in mud and torn in places. Ruined beyond repair. Just like her marriage. Silly to think a dress, bobbed hair, and a chicken dinner would change Henry's heart toward her.

She tried to wiggle her toes. It was hopeless. Even if she could wiggle them, how would she know? She couldn't see them, and she couldn't feel her legs. She struggled to sit up, but the weight of gravity pulled her back. Wiping her face, she wrestled to get free, but she couldn't budge.

Tilting her chin to look behind her, she twisted to swipe her arm down as far as she could stretch. She couldn't reach the stream. The water hadn't gotten to her yet, but in this downpour, the level had to be rising. It was only a matter of time before it filled the ditch she was lying in, head first.

More likely she'd die from the cold or loss of blood first. For all she knew, her legs had been cut off or mangled, and she was bleeding to death.

"Oh, Henry." She placed her hand on her stomach to quell the nausea. "Please come find me. Even if you don't love me, rescue me again."

*****

Henry had searched until his flashlight battery ran out. All he could do was rest against an old elm tree and wait until morning. He tried to close his eyes and get some sleep, but even if the rain hadn't been pouring down on him all night, he wouldn't have been able. Too worried about Vivian. All he could manage was to cry out to God. He tried to pray the Lord's will be done, but instead, he begged to be able to find her alive.

If God would give him a second chance, he'd be the kind of husband she deserved, not the man his father was. He would show her how much she meant to him. Even if she didn't have any respect left for him, he would spend the rest of his life loving and cherishing her just as he vowed on their wedding day.

After a long miserable night, the sun shone through the clouds, and the rain stopped, but the dark clouds showed it would start up again soon. At least now he could see the path in front of him. He moved at a faster pace to get to the church, sometimes running, sometimes slowing his pace to a brisk walk until he could run again. If he could borrow Reverend Krieger's horse, it might help with the search.

Branches were strewn over the fields, trees broken off halfway up. They had been snapped in two. He passed a barn, at least it looked like it might have been a barn, that had crumbled in a heap of wood. An outhouse rested on top of a black Hudson automobile where the twister must have dropped it. The sheriff owned a car like that.

A grove of maple trees ahead hadn't been touched by the storm and stood about fifty feet from the church. He raced over the hill toward the building, but it wasn't there. The roof and walls had blown away leaving only the wooden cross standing among the rubble.

Heaviness weighted on his chest. He'd wasted time trying to get here while Vivian was out there somewhere. He should have realized there would be nobody here to help. He'd failed her again.

What if the storm hit during church last night? Thirty to forty people would have been there, maybe killed by the twister's path, but wouldn't people be here trying to dig out any survivors? It probably hit before anyone got there or after everyone went home.

The parsonage. He blew out his breath. The pastor's house, a green bungalow with a couple of shingles blown off the roof, was still intact on the other side of the field. He ran toward it and knocked on the door.

Reverend Krieger's soft wrinkles imbedded in his face as he answered the door. "Henry! Come on in, son. I'm so glad you made it through the storm."

"Reverend." Henry stepped inside where Mrs. Krieger tried to take his coat. "I can't stay. Vivian's missing. I need to find her. Can I borrow your horse?"

"Say no more." Reverend Krieger slipped on his overcoat. "I'll saddle him for you."

Henry stuck his hand in his pocket fumbling for some change. "I can pay you."

"Henry Bauer." Mrs. Krieger thumped his chest with her finger. "You won't pay us a dime, you hear!"

He almost refused, but he needed to find Vivian. "Thank you." His voice cracked.

Reverend Krieger placed a hand on Henry's shoulder. "There are other men out looking for survivors. Maybe one of them found her."

"Where would she be if they did?"

"They made a make-shift hospital at the schoolhouse," the reverend said. "You should check there first. Most of the men have gone there to form search parties. I'm sure they'd help you look."

Don't accept nothing from nobody, boy.

Henry shook himself to get his father's voice out of his head. He would take whatever help he could get to find Vivian in time to save her. "I'll bring your horse back when I find her."

He helped the reverend saddle the chestnut horse and galloped west, in the direction of the school. Even with the storm damage, he was making good time. He passed a house in ruins, and his stomach knotted. It was the Weber's farm, but he couldn't take the time to stop.

"Help."

Henry pulled up the reins and listened. Maybe he imagined the voice.

"Help."

It was a child. He heard it call out again. The little girl's voice had come from the house. He bit his lip. Help was at the schoolhouse. Other men could rescue whoever it was.

Flicking the reins and rode about two feet. What if it had been his child? He pulled back on the reins. Dismounting the horse, he ran to the pile of rubble.

The sound came from where pieces of wood formed a heap. He waited for a moment while he tried to figure out how to remove the wood without making the pile collapse.

Holding his breath, he pulled away a top piece.

"Help."

"It's all right. I'm here." He carefully removed a few more

pieces as quickly as he could without causing the structure to fall. One more piece and a hand slipped out.

He tossed away some more planks and pulled seven-year-old Rebecca Weber out of the wreckage. She was dirty, and her blond braids were unraveling. "Are you hurt?"

"I don't think so." Her voice sounded weak.

He kneeled down and wiped a tear from her face. "Honey, where's your parents and your brothers and sisters?"

"I don't know." Rebecca sobbed on his shoulder, and he let her.

When her sobs waned, he picked her up and carried her to the horse. "We need to get help. You can come with me to the schoolhouse."

He didn't know if Rebecca heard him because she didn't respond, didn't even look his direction. When he lifted her on the horse, she let out a whimper but didn't say anything more.

Mounted behind her, he held her tight. They rode past a couple of other houses hit by the twister, but he didn't stop. He needed to get her someplace safe. Besides, he couldn't do anything by himself. As they rode, he uttered a prayer they would find the help they needed in time.

Chapter Fifteen

With dreams of swirling clouds chasing her, Vivian woke with a start. Sunlight glimmered on the horizon, but she couldn't see anyone. Maybe Henry didn't bother to look.

No, she couldn't give up hope. He'd come for her just like he did a year ago.

She tilted her head back to see if the rain in the ditch had risen. It was maybe six inches away. Gasping, she looked toward the sky. The rain had stopped, but dark clouds threatened. If it rained hard again, she might drown before he found her.

A turkey vulture landed on the branch resting on Vivian's legs, waiting for her to take her last breath. She screamed and waved at it, and it flew away, but it would be back. Maybe next time, it would have a good meal.

"No!" Henry would get there first. She had to hold onto that thought.

He didn't even love her. Hadn't he tried to save her from the tornado? He tried to hold on.

She squeezed her eyes shut.

He would come for her. He wouldn't give up.

*****

A tree had crashed into the side of the schoolhouse, but a tent had been erected nearby. A group of men piled supplies into the back of a pick-up truck. Henry ignored them, took Rebecca into his arms, and rushed into the tent.

Doctor Oster kneeled on the ground wrapping a bandage around a boy's arm. The boy cried as his mother sat by his side comforting him. A few other women, including the doctor's wife, Nadine Zimmer, and Hope Hahn, rolled bandages in the corner.

Vivian wasn't there.

Mrs. Oster bustled to his side and took Rebecca from his arms. "What happened? Isn't that one of the Weber girls?"

"I found her buried under a pile of rubble."

"It's good you brought her here." Hope dipped a rag in a basin of water. "Shhh, Rebecca, it's all right. You're safe now. She started wiping the dirt off Rebecca's forehead then turned to Henry. "What happened to the rest of them?"

A twinge of guilt knotted Henry's stomach. "I don't know. I thought I should get Rebecca here, maybe get help to dig them out."

"The sheriff's gathered some men outside," Mrs. Oster said. "Best you let him know what happened."

Henry opened the tent flap but stopped before he stepped outside, said, "Has anyone seen Vivian?"

"No," Mrs. Oster said. "Did you two get separated?"

"She…" Henry wiped a hand through his hair. "The storm. She blew away."

Mrs. Oster splayed her hand over her mouth.

"She's not dead." It came out a little harsher than Henry intended.

"I'm sure the men will find her." Mrs. Oster's said.

Henry nodded and pushed through the door.

Some men who he knew in passing, but hadn't spent time getting acquainted with, had finished loading up when he headed toward them. The only man he'd spent any time with was Archie Hahn. Nate Johnson, Hank Andrews, and Ben Tanner. They had farms within a couple miles of his. Everyone had come out to help their neighbors during this time of crisis.

If Vivian were safe, would he have been here to help? His past indifference hit him like a strong wind causing him to step back. *God, I'm so sorry.*

Abe Zimmer came toward him, and for the first time, seeing him gave Henry a sense of relief.

"Sheriff Abe." Henry shook his hand. "I'd like to join the search team. I have Reverend Krieger's horse."

"We'd be glad to have you," the sheriff said. "Did you run across anyone in need on the way in?"

"The Weber house collapsed. I dug one of their girls out, but I don't know where her folks or the other children are. The Cooper's and the Dyson's houses are wrecked too."

"Cooper and Dyson have already stopped by," Sheriff Abe said. "Not a scratch on them or their kin. I was worried when Jeff didn't show up at the school. Anyone else?"

Henry swallowed hard. "Vivian's missing. We need to find

her."

"How she'd get away from you?" The sheriff didn't say it in an accusing way.

He didn't have to. Henry blamed himself enough for both of them. His voice thickened. "The twister took her."

"We go to the Weber's house first," Sheriff Abe said. "Then we'll find your misses."

Everything in Henry wanted to rant. As ashamed as he was of his attitude, he didn't want to help the Webers or anyone else. He wanted to find his wife. As much as it pained him to admit it, Abe was right. They needed to try to get the children out of what was left of the house before it collapsed on them.

Even after the way he acted, they wouldn't hesitate to help him find Vivian. He needed their help, so he nodded, mounted the chestnut, and tried to ignore the knot in his gut.

They would find the Weber children and their parents alive, and then they'd rescue Vivian in time. He had to keep believing.

*****

Vivian woke shivering. Even in the middle of winter, she'd never remembered being this cold. Her teeth rattled, and she couldn't get them to stop. If only she had a blanket.

Or a drink of water.

Her throat was so dry it hurt to swallow.

She locked in the ditch. There was plenty of rain water there. If she could reach, maybe she could bring a handful of water and bring it to her lips.

Stretching her arm out, she tried it. The water was just below where she could reach. She tried to move the upper part of her body a little, but it didn't work.

Her teeth chattered as another shiver jolted through her.

What was taking Henry so long? She couldn't take the cold and thirst much longer.

Dizziness swept over her, and she closed her eyes to keep the spinning at bay. Nausea overwhelmed her, and she turned her head to vomit. A drop of water pelted her cheek. Then another. A gentle shower at first, then a hard rain.

Time was running out.

Her vision blurred. She remembered another time when she was lost and in trouble.

*****

She was six years old and had wandered away from the picnic area. Mom told her not to go too far, but she was so fascinated by the brightly colored leaves falling off the trees she didn't listen.

A squirrel ran past into the woods and up a tree. She squealed and followed after it. A deer stood watching her a ways further. She started toward it, but it skirted away. Then she sat in the middle of a pile of yellow leaves and threw them up in the air. It looked like it was raining yellow. She threw them up again, then buried herself in them, and went to sleep.

When she woke, it was dark. The moon cast shadows on the bare trees making them look like scary animals in the fairytale books Daddy read.

She didn't know which way to go. She couldn't even find the path.

"Daddy!" Tears poured from her eyes. "Daddy!"

Crickets chirped and an owl hooted. She had heard these sounds before, many times, lying safe in her bed at night, but these sounded different. Scary. Like they wanted to eat her.

Vivian ran. Something caught her dress, and she was afraid it was a wild animal trying to attack her. She pulled away and ripped her sleeve on a tree branch. Mom would yell at her. She warned her to be careful not to tear her clothes.

An alcove of rocks up ahead seemed like a safe place to hide. Unless there was a bear or a snake. She drew closer looking for signs of danger, but nothing was there. She curled up in a ball and cried.

"God, please let my daddy find me."

"Vivian!" A man's voice called through the darkness. "Vivian!"

"Daddy, I'm over here."

*****

Vivian wiped a tear from her eyes. It had been a long time since she trusted God enough to pray like she did when she was lost in the woods. It wasn't long after that her father got involved in gambling and drinking. He wasn't around much, but when he was home, she and her sisters would hear her mom and dad arguing late into the night.

It had been her fault. If she hadn't been so much trouble

getting lost, her daddy would still be around. She still had hope he would come home one day and take her on a picnic or a hike through the woods like he used to, but it never happened. He didn't love her anymore.

When James fell in love with her, she started to believe someone could love her, maybe God even cared for her. He seemed so close to her then, but when James died in the war and her parents and sisters died during the epidemic and left her alone, she gave up.

She'd given up hope.

Then God sent Henry to rescue her. Why else would he show up on the very day she was going to end it all and ask her to marry him?

Maybe God had been looking out for her all this time, and she hadn't even realized it. She'd been looking to Henry to fill a hole in her heart only the Holy Spirit could heal.

"Lord, I'm sorry I didn't trust you. Please help me. Show Henry where to look for me."

She looked back. The water in the ditch had risen an inch.

"Lord, please hurry."

*****

Henry flicked the reins of the horse as the rope tied to the saddle pulled a heavy beam off the Weber house. They'd been at it now for hours, and the rain was starting to pick up. If they didn't find the Weber children soon, he'd have to go looking for Vivian on his own.

"Pull harder," Sheriff Abe called out. "A little bit more."

The beam pulled loose, and Henry dismounted. He and the men who were with him drug debris out of the way.

Sheriff Abe took a pick axe and slammed it into the area they were clearing. He made a hole big enough to lower himself in. "Anyone there."

A groan sounded.

"Henry, you come with me." The sheriff barked out his orders.

Henry caught a glimpse of the man Abe had become over the last few years, the hero who had won all those medals during the Great War. He wasn't the braggart, Henry thought he was. He took on the leadership role with humility and compassion and did what needed to be done.

"Hank, take Henry's place on the horse. Jeff, grab some of those shovels, and the rest of you, keep digging."

Henry waited for Sheriff Abe to lower himself through the hole, and then followed. Dirty water drizzled on his head, but he couldn't see anything. He pulled the flashlight, now equipped with new batteries, from his belt hook and shone it into the hole.

An opening, almost like a room underground had formed, untouched by the wreckage above. Sheriff Abe motioned him to shine the light closer. Another groan sounded as the light flashed on two little girls with a wardrobe on top of them. Three of their brothers were trying to pull it off of them, but it wouldn't budge. Henry set the flashlight down and grabbed one end of the wardrobe while Abe grabbed the other and lifted it off the girls.

"Are you all right?" Abe asked as he lifted one of the girls and handed her to Henry.

"It hurts."

"Archie," Henry called. "We found five of them."

Archie reached down and took the girl from Henry. Abe handed Henry the other girl. She gave him a wide-eyed stare. Henry lifted her up to Archie then helped the boys squeeze through the hole.

"We need to find the rest of them," the sheriff said.

Henry's stomach knotted. "If they're not here, they were buried in this mess or blown away. I need to find my wife."

Abe placed a hand on Henry's shoulder. "You saw the twister take her. She's gone. These people might still be alive."

"Vivian's not dead." He swiped Abe's hand away and tried to calm the panicked tone in his voice. "She's out there waiting for me to find her."

"You don't even know where to look."

"I have to try."

Abe blew out a noisy sigh. "Look, you help us dig out the rest of this family, and we'll all help you look for Vivian. Got it?"

Henry jaw quivered. If he thought he could find his wife without their help, he'd tell Abe he was on his own. He gave a curt nod and grabbed a shovel.

*****

If the sun had been shining, it would have been halfway

across the sky by now. It had to be one or two o'clock in the afternoon by now with no sign of the rain stopping. They'd been digging for hours and the only thing they'd found was Jeff Weber's body crushed under the debris.

A heaviness rested on Henry's chest. Five children would grow up without their parents, and four more would never see another day.

He strode toward the sheriff. "We need to look for my wife now."

Sheriff Abe threw some shovels onto the truck. "We'll get to it. We need to take the children back to the school for medical treatment."

Henry rubbed his temples. "Archie can take them back while the rest of us start looking."

Abe's brow furrowed. His eyes darted toward the crew. "Henry, the men need some rest. We've been digging those people out for hours." He leaned against the car. "We'll help you look after we get something to eat, but you have to understand, your wife is gone. It may be days before we find the body."

Henry grabbed Abe's collar. "She's not dead, I tell you. We need to find her."

Abe glanced at Henry's hands. The others stood gaping as if he had lost his wits.

Henry let go and turned away. How could he convince this man he'd always looked on with suspicion he wasn't crazy, God showed him Vivian was alive? He swiped at the tears forming in his eyes and turned back toward the sheriff. "Please. Please help me find her."

Abe's lips pressed together in a slight grimace. Then he nodded. "Archie, take the men back to the school to get some lunch. Then meet Henry and me at…" His look darted toward Henry. "Where'd you last see her?"

"At the grove of maple trees half mile from the church."

"We'll be about a half mile east of the church. After you eat, try to catch up with us."

Archie stepped forward, his eyes blank with a distant stare. "I don't know about the rest of the men, Abe, but I don't need nothing to eat." His voice had a soft tone like he had been too drained by the tragedy to put much effort forward to speak. "I'll be back as soon as we drop off the children and let Hope…" He cleared his throat. "Let Hope know what happened."

"Me too," Hank said.

"My wife's been trying to get me to eat less anyway," Ben said as he patted his stomach.

"Well, I'm not eating alone," Nate said. "I'll be back too."

Henry throat grew thick. Maybe he should have spent time getting to know these men. After the way he acted toward them, they were still willing to help him.

Abe placed a hand on Henry's shoulder. "If she's alive, we'll find her."

"Let's hurry up," Nate said as the men climbed into the truck.

"Now," Abe said. "Let's get moving."

Henry mounted his horse when he heard a cry from behind him. "Quiet," he yelled. "I think I hear something."

The men all stopped what they were doing and listened. The cry grew louder, and Henry and Abe ran toward the bushes where the sound came from. Henry stopped short. There, behind an elderberry shrub laid Rose Weber's body with Frank, her four-month-old son, squirming beside her.

Abe ran to the baby and picked him up. " Near as I can figure, the tornado picked them up. Rose must have shielded her son when they fell."

Archie rushed to them, took Frank, and the baby stopped crying. "How could she have held on to him?"

"It's a miracle." The sheriff turned to Henry. "If God can protect this baby, maybe Vivian is alive. Let's go find out."

A rush of adrenalin flowed through Henry as he mounted his horse. He rode ahead and led Abe's police car to the grove where his Model T sat stuck with its front right tire in the ditch. When they arrived, he gazed across the area as he dismounted and ran to the spot where Vivian had been taken from him.

He scanned the road then the wooded areas on either side. Too many directions. He didn't know where to look.

"The storm came from the west." Abe's voice startled him. "We need to head east, in the direction of the church."

"I tried looking last night." Henry wiped his face with his handkerchief. "It was so dark, and the batteries in my flashlight died. Maybe I miss something." He looked to the east, but something seemed off. Somehow, he knew he wouldn't find her there. "We need to look that way." He pointed to the broken trees west of them.

Abe rubbed his chin. "We won't find her there. We need to follow the path the tornado took."

What the sheriff said made sense. Henry knew it was the wise thing to do, but he couldn't shake the feeling the he needed to look west. He set his face and started walking.

"Henry." Abe ran after him. "You're going the wrong way."

The muscle in Henry's jaw twitched. "I know the Holy Spirit is telling me to look this way. You don't have to come."

"What if you're wrong?"

Henry swallowed. "I can't worry about it right now."

"All right." Abe hurried to catch up with him. "I hope you're right."

"So do I," Henry said. "So do I."

Chapter Sixteen

Vivian didn't know how long she'd been out of it this time, but she sensed it had been a couple of hours. She didn't have to stretch her head back to know it had been steadily raining and the water had risen. Her hair, forehead, and ears were already doused. If she fell asleep again, she would drown.

It didn't really matter. She didn't have enough strength left to hold her head up. It was only a matter of time before the water covered her nose and mouth.

Death was close at hand. She couldn't help but feel sad because Henry would never know how much she truly loved and respected him. He was her knight in shining armor from the fairytales of her childhood. Unlike her father, he had rescued her from a life of pain and misery. She'd been so grateful to him.

Her deepest regret was she'd spent so much time believing Jesus didn't love her when He'd been there all along. The greatest thing He'd done other than dying on the cross for her sin was sending Henry to her.

Lord, take care of Henry for me.

She couldn't fight to stay awake any longer. As she drifted off, knowing she'd soon be in Heaven, she heard Henry calling her name.

*****

"Vivian! Vivian!" Henry ran toward the ditch where his wife lay, the water covering her face. "Vivian." When he reached her, he plopped in the flooded ditch and lifted her head out.

She coughed and spit out water.

"Thank God." She was alive.

Sheriff Abe dashed toward them and examined the tree branch across her legs.

A knot formed in Henry's stomach. "How are her legs? Are they…"

"They don't look bad, maybe broken." Abe leaned over and tested the weight of the limb. "We need to get this branch off of her and get her out of this ditch before she drowns."

Henry stroked her head. "Vivian, can you hear me?"

"Henry." Her voice was weak. "You came for me. I knew you would."

"I love you." Henry's voice thickened. "I've always loved you."

"Henry, I..."

"Save your strength, darling. We'll get you out of here."

"Mrs. Bauer," Sheriff Abe said. "Do you think you could hold your head out of the water without Henry's help?"

"I'll try."

Henry eased her down, but she couldn't hold her head up. Before her face went under, he grabbed hold of her again.

"I can't lift this on my own," the sheriff said.

Henry swallowed. "If I let go, she'll drown."

"I'll get the others." Abe started toward his car. "I'll be back as soon as I can."

"Hurry," Henry called after him. He sat in the water under his wife and allowed her head to rest on his chest. "It'll be all right. He'll be back soon."

She didn't say anything, but her head sank into him as she closed her eyes.

The rain had drenched her auburn hair and the mud saturated her, but she never looked more beautiful. He couldn't believe the argument they had yesterday. Why hadn't he told her how pretty she was in her dress and hairstyle, how desirable?

"You're so beautiful."

Her eyes sprang open.

"Shh. Everything will be all right."

"Henry." It came out as a whisper.

"Don't talk. I'm here. Just rest."

"Have to." She paused for so long he thought she might have decided to rest like he told her. "I'm sorry. I... I love you too."

A warmth traveled through him. He wanted to believe her, but he knew better. She was hurt. That's why she said it.

"I do." She struggled to turn toward him. "You came for me. You always..." She closed her eyes.

His heart dropped as he leaned closer to see if she was breathing. Her warm breath on his cheek eased his fears. He stroked her hair as she rested on him. Maybe she did love him, at least a little. He determined she would never again doubt his love for her again.

Suddenly, the rain stopped, and the clouds parted allowing the sun to shine through. Before he even realized what was happening, his neighbors surrounded him pulling the tree limb from her legs. He lifted her out of the mud and water and carried her to the sheriff's car.

"Ben," Henry said. "Would you mind taking Reverend Krieger his horse? I'd like to ride with my wife."

Ben nodded.

He had asked so many favors today, favors he'd never be able to repay. He didn't care. These men were his neighbors, and after today, he would offer his friendship to them. Accepting help to take care of his wife wasn't weakness or failure. It was strength.

*****

Henry tried to convince Doctor Oster to allow him to stay, but the doctor ordered him to leave the tent. Sheriff Abe grabbed hold of his arm and escorted him out. "Henry, the doctor can't do her much good with you in the way."

After pacing for half an hour, he stopped and leaned against a nearby tree.

Abe came over and stood beside him. "The Weber children are doing fine except for a few cuts and bruises. Archie took them home with him. He and Hope are going to raise them."

Henry's face flushed. He hadn't even bothered to ask how the children they'd rescued earlier were doing. All he could think about was Vivian. "That's good."

Silence filled the air between them for a long while.

"Sherriff Abe, what you did back there…" Henry cleared his throat. "I owe you an apology for the way I've acted."

"Apology accepted." Abe shook his hand. "You were right about looking to the west."

"I can't explain it." Henry looked toward Heaven. "It's like God showed me she was alive and where to look."

Doctor Oster came out of the tent, and Henry rushed up to him. "Is she all right? Can I see her?"

"Two broken legs and some bruises, but she'll be fine. Good thing you found her when you did. Hypothermia was starting to set in. I set her legs in plaster casts, and she'll need plenty of rest and blankets to keep her warm, but time heals all wounds, even broken legs."

Henry let out a breath he didn't even realize he was holding and entered the tent. Time may heal broken legs, but only God could heal their broken marriage.

Vivian lay on a cot with at least five blankets over her. When she glanced up and smiled, warmth swept through him. He couldn't imagine whatever possessed him to think about leaving her. He knelt at her side and reached under the blankets to take her hand in his. "I love you so much. I'm so sorry I haven't told you before, but you're going to hear it every day from this moment on."

She licked her lips. "I knew you would come for me." Her voice sounded weak.

"I'm going to try to change, to be the husband you want me to be. Someday, I'll be the kind of man you can love and respect, someone like James."

Vivian squeezed his hand tighter. "You're my husband, and I love you."

Henry's jaw twitched. "What about James?"

"A part of me will always think fondly of him. He was my first love, but you're the man God sent to rescue me, my knight in shining armor, the man I want to spend the rest of my life with."

Henry leaned down to kiss his wife.

*****

On Easter Sunday, Vivian sat in the passenger seat of their Model T as Henry drove to the field where Resurrection of Hope Church once stood. She was amazed her husband so readily accepted Abe's help to dig his automobile out of the ditch earlier that week. He and the sheriff even sat on the porch afterwards and played a game of checkers.

Henry had voiced concern Vivian wasn't up to going to church, but she didn't want to miss this Resurrection Sunday. Today was a double celebration, the resurrection of Christ from the dead and the resurrection of her marriage.

He parked next to three other Model Ts and untied the wheelchair from the roof where he had secured it. After lifting her out of the car, he set her in the chair before wheeling her to the field where the debris from the church had been removed.

Archie stepped over to greet them, but Hope stayed with the

children, holding the baby in her arms as if she couldn't bear to go even a few feet away from them.

A few days ago, Henry had helped his neighbors bury those who died in the tornado. When he came home, he sobbed in Vivian's arms, and it almost frightened her. She never expected he could show so much emotion.

"How are the children?" Henry asked.

"As good as can be expected," Archie said. "Hope wants to bring them over to your house tomorrow to visit. Since us menfolk are going to be working on building the new church, I thought it might be a good idea."

Vivian's stomach fluttered. "I'd love it."

Henry grabbed her hand. "You sure you're up to it? I could stay home and take care of you."

"You go help your friends." She squeezed his hand. "I'll be fine.

He touched her cheek. "I love you."

Warmth flushed her face. Since the tornado, the words had poured out of her husband often. He had told her he'd always loved her, even when she was with James.

"I didn't marry you because of the promise I made. I married you because I love and adore you. I always have, and I always will."

She had started to believe him. It astounded her how God had shown His love for her through her husband.

It wasn't only his words. Henry had started showing affection for her in small ways, and he'd moved back into the bedroom.

Reverend Krieger cleared his throat. "This has been a hard week on all of us. Some among us are no longer here. They've gone to be with the Lord who is the Resurrection and the Life. Let this not be a day of grief, but of gladness as we remember the hope Christ's resurrection brings."

The reverend lifted his hands toward Heaven. "Christ is risen!" He motioned for the others to respond.

"Christ is risen indeed!"

About the Author

Tamera Lynn Kraft has always loved adventures. She loves to write historical fiction set in the United States because there are so many stories in American history. There are strong elements of faith, romance, suspense and adventure in her stories. She has received 2nd place in the NOCW contest, 3rd place TARA writer's contest, and is a finalist in the Frasier Writing Contest.

Tamera been married for thirty-nine years to the love of her life, Rick, and has two married adult children and three grandchildren. She has been a children's pastor for over twenty years. She is the leader of a ministry called Revival Fire for Kids where she mentors other children's leaders, teaches workshops, and is a children's ministry consultant and children's evangelist and has written children's church curriculum. She is a recipient of the 2007 National Children's Leaders Association Shepherd's Cup for lifetime achievement in children's ministry.

You can contact Tamera online at her website: *http://tameralynnkraft.net*

www.ingramcontent.com/pod-product-compliance
Lightning Source LLC
Chambersburg PA
CBHW032048180726
48284CB00004B/1241